Kareen Lopez-Samuels hails from the small island of Jamaica and currently resides in Brampton, Ontario with her family members. A teacher of English by profession who was formally trained at The Mico University College and has been an educator for over 20 years. She is the author of *Zimera, They Were Here Before, Rescued from Myself and Temperate Eventually Learns a Lesson* (a children's book). She lovingly refers to these as *The Pandemic Chronicles* as they were written and published between December 2019 and January 2022. The first child and only girl for her parents Winston Lopez and Beatrice Stone Lopez; although Beatrice transitioned when Kareen was only 17 years old, her teachings and way of being remain a constant source of great inspiration. She completed a BA in Linguistics from UWI (Mona, Jamaica), an MA in Language, Culture & Education and an Honours Specialist in English from York University. She is currently employed to the Peel District School Board.

This book is dedicated to my mom (deceased), dad, husband, my two girls, all my brothers, Ann Marie Steele Daley, Tashna Servis-Morris (my sisters and friends); all my relatives and friends, for all their love. I consider myself blessed beyond measure to have each and every one of you in my life. My greatest desire is that this book brings healing in families. I am grateful that my parents inspired a love for reading in me from a very early age, my dad always bought me literature books and I always had "free time" to read. I am beyond grateful.

Kareen Lopez-Samuels

EMERSYN

A Tale in Being Prudent

AUSTIN MACAULEY PUBLISHERS™

LONDON * CAMBRIDGE * NEW YORK * SHARJAH

A CIP catalogue record for this title is available from the British Library.

ISBN 9781398441651 (Paperback)
ISBN 9781398441668 (ePub e-book)

www.austinmacauley.com

First Published 2023
Austin Macauley Publishers Ltd®
1 Canada Square
Canary Wharf
London
E14 5AA

I am eternally grateful to all the people who have encouraged me in one way or the next; literally, too numerous to mention, but you know yourselves so take a bow. To all the people who have inspired me; keep on shining, sometimes the rest of us need your light to find our way. Thank you, Marva Waugh, John "Toby" Cadham, Saundra Fisher, Gail Bogle, Nadia Nembhard-Hunt, Courace Fisher and Barbara Stewart-Edwards for your constant and consistent encouragement you are appreciated.

Table of Contents

Introduction

I AM ONLY HUMAN
I laugh and I cry
I slip and I slide
But I still continue to try.
I am only human.
I fall, I bleed,
I bruise, I heal.
I hate, I love.
Invariably, I am only human.
I have strong emotions and opinions.
Some I feel inherently connected to, others fade with the setting sun.
Time after time, I am hated, I am loved!
Can you tell that I am only human?
I often chide to hide the pain.
When I feel like I'll never breathe again,
I lash out and speak aloud,
Don't judge me! Don't you see that I am only human?
Like a tiger caught in a trap,
I won't be held back.
At those times, my actions are racialised so they can be politicised
I'll never know why because I am only human.
If I am only human, why does my skin tone inspire hate?
Why does the width of my nose and the volume of my thighs get some people high?
You know why?
It serves their purpose: to divide, to ostracise, to further minimise.
Look again because it is not always about race and engendering strife.
It is more so about taking up space.

But we've been hardwired to see faces, in places where a soul should dwell.
Therefore, we must unlearn to relearn how to tap into souls.
Ultimately and irrevocably, I am only human.
So, pick a side, choose humanity
Just try because you know why?
You and I are only human.

Part One

Chapter One
The Whileys

"Generation to generation... and from there, back to the stars that birthed them. A perfect circle." – Amie Kaufman

Mason

We live in Shrove, a small town, almost like an alcove, in the most southern part of the most southern state. Living in this alcove; therefore, means that we are protected from a lot of the elements. For instance, in all our history, we have never suffered destruction from a tornado or a hurricane. Shrove was settled in the late seventeen hundred by a military genius called Thomas Shrove; hence the name. Shrove was a general in the United States Army and served his country well, with pride and honour. He was said to be a great man of integrity. It is often rumoured that both him and his younger brother Richard, took on hundreds of Native Indians and won; thereby, winning this spot of ground fair and square. But then again, how could you *not* win when you have the more advance weaponry?

The people of Shrove are deeply religious and being a small town, everyone knows everyone. There are no secrets among us, if there is, maybe just one person is privy to that tale. We have a few Christian denominations but mostly we stick to the same fundamental doctrine '*Do unto thy neighbour as you would have them do unto you*'. We believe that a number of the world's problems could be solved by this central truth as people would be quicker to withhold vengeance if this vengeance would be reimbursed to their credit. A cardinal truth that if utilised effectively can spare everyone heartache and pain. It is as simple as that and a well-known fact in these parts! Also, no fancy talking, as primarily we are a simple people; hence, not given to much fanfare. No, we are definitely not an ostentatious bunch. What you see is usually what you get and we thrive on always being prudent. However, people being people, there are some exceptions to this rule as there are those who covet but they always suffer as a consequence.

The temperature here in Shrove is always mild even when it snows. Almost every type of cultivated plant is able to grow here. We have indeed been blessed with a rich silt soil that is both dark and lovely and rich in vitamins for optimal growth. My family have been farmers in these parts for as far back as the time of Shrove itself. In fact, there is mention in our family's archive that my mama is a direct descendant from the Shrove lineage. It is written in our family's records, as plain as day, for all our descendants to see and therefore know that they are derived from greatness. Opportunely, all our accomplishments, sorrow and goals have been written in *The Whiley Chronicles*, for posterity.

My mama, being a descendant of this great man, is a great strategist in her own right and is a constant in my daily life. I cannot begin to imagine what I will do without her. Life just won't be the same.

Another valuable piece of advice that mama taught me is never to acquiesce to anyone unless there is hope for my survival. Never mind that this is the same person who always gave her time and energy to all and sundry. I often asked her why and her response has never wavered.

"For posterity, boy! This family has seen its fair share of struggles and hardships so anything I can do to alleviate that, I will!"

And without wavering she always adds, "And you should too."

Also, from when I was a little tadpole, she used to say to me, "Mason, always be sure to keep your wits about you and never allow your emotions to lead you astray. Many men have lost everything because they could never reign in their emotions; could never be prudent."

She's been telling me this, as far back as I can remember and always with the exact same expression on her face. An expression of faraway places, lost dreams and broken promises set against the backdrop of sparkling blue eyes. Mama was and still is a natural beauty, these new age women with their false lashes, facial contours and filters have nothing on her. Of course, her sad eyes no longer sparkle as they used to but she is still as much the prom queen my daddy married over fifty years ago.

My daddy's name is Cahal and my mum is Beatrice. My dad went home to be with the Lord seven years ago and I don't think Mama has fully recovered from this. She still wears her widows' garb – full black dress, complete with a mesh head covering. As a result, Mum holds dear to my father's ideas to honour him in his absence and this makes her even more non-compliant as she is being stubborn for two. Traditionally, in our family the eldest son is generally left in charge, so I am in charge of the house, the property, all the day to day operations of the family and all the business decisions. Daddy used to refer to my mum as his *apple blossom* not simply because of her rich complexion but also because our apple orchard is our most prized possession.

This orchard has been in our family since before the time of Andrew Johnson, the seventeenth president of United States, who came to office after the assassination of Abraham Lincoln. Johnson was in power for just one term from (1865–1869). This goes to show how long we've had our orchard. However, before this time, we had always cultivated cotton and maize; in addition, to chickens – so happy we don't have chickens anymore – the smell must have been nauseating. Johnson was inaugurated at the end of the *American Civil War* (April 12, 1861 to May 9, 1865) which is when my great, great, great, great, granddaddy (Lance Jr Whiley) lost the right to own slaves.

Here in the south, many families have long since sold their properties and either moved away or have invested in less agrarian ventures but our property has been in the Whiley family for generations. Shrove has seen her fair share of ups and downs as well. She is currently booming and the Whileys have a great hand in that. Much like Shrove, our family has faced much misfortune but through it all we have been constrained by our ancestors to preserve our inheritance as custodians of our cultural beliefs and practices. We have always come out on the other side no matter what assails us and have accumulated enough wealth through our various holdings and interests to last a life-time. Obviously, we fully intend to keep this tradition going because as the good Book says, '*A good man leaves an inheritance to his children's children.*'

However, as rich as our property is, it is not the sole prize in our family. No, sir! The family house sits on a little hill overseeing acres and acres of rich farmland; prime real estate and seated behind her; like a permanent, imposing, magnificent frame, stands a picturesque mountain of rolling hills; emerald green in the summer, hues of green, yellow and brown in the fall seasons and glorious whites in the winter. We have long since claimed this mountain as our own property and since there is no specific laws on the books about private citizens owning mountains, it will remain in our family for decades to come.

We call our home Emersyn. My great, great, great, great, great, great, great, grandmother (Babs) was a hopeless romantic in her day and she thought Emersyn had a certain majestic ring to it. Plus, the natural greenery that surrounds Emersyn and the rich colour which adorns her is a true testament to the pertinence of the name. Needless to say, our family's emblem is the emerald gemstone, not only because of its rich hue but its strength and endurance which represent us as a people. Significantly, it is from Emersyn that I inherited my name Mason. Of course, Emersyn was not the original name. The previous owners called it something else, but at this point, no one can remember what it used to be called. It is one of those things where once Emersyn was established, no one can remember anything that existed prior to her perpetuity.

Since this is indeed the family house, all my siblings live here as well, it is an unspoken rule that we all remain in the family house until we die and the next in line takes over. This has been the Whiley way for as far back as the day Emersyn was acquired. Mind you, only family members can live here, or stay here there is a strict policy of no outsiders. We protect our privacy at all cost and abhor any intrusion.

I have four brothers and two sisters; in total there are seven of us. A huge family indeed by any standard. In order of appearance, there is me, Emery, Gabriel, Amethyst and Melisandre (fraternal twins) who are inseparable, Valencia and my youngest brother Everest. Yes, we are quite a brood and our temperaments as diverse as our names. Among us we have an average of two to three kids except for Valencia and Everest. Valencia never got married – or not yet – and Everest is married to a daring wildcat named Andira. Everest, himself, is like a volcano in his anger, not a quiet, sleeping one either but fierce and explosive in his rage. He has always been this way ever since he was little. Both him and Andira fight constantly and consistently, always yelling and breaking things, so far, they have broken a total of three heirlooms which are irreplaceable, broke Mama's heart to part with some of her prized possessions. It is therefore no surprise to any of us that there are no babies. How could there be?

Of necessity, we are a very tightknit family. Each Whiley has a role to play in advancing the many and various business interests of the family. Obviously, we prefer to keep everything within the family, it is just the way we prefer to take care of our dynasty; not to mention, it is just being prudent. Among our many business enterprises, we have a winery (wine made from our unique apples), along with a non-alcoholic variety. We have marketed our name as a brand so we are *locally owned with an international flare*. We have a marketing and communication company, we do business with local entrepreneurs, people out of state as well and with companies as far away as Europe. There is a commerce arm to our business dealings which covers accounting. A firm that does our personal and business accounts and those of the local farmers who can't be bothered with the complexities of the accounting aspect of the business. The Whileys also have shares in international and local businesses; such as, the Shrove Newspaper and one of the four radio and television stations in the town.

By way of the division of labour the twins are in charge of all things marketing, Amethyst has become the face of the Whiley brand with his gorgeous green eyes being a staple on all our advertisements. The one thing we all know about Amethyst is that he is fiercely ambitious and self-serving but he is the best man for the job and sometimes as a leader, one has to just do what will yield the most favourable results despite the conditions. Also, I refuse to make the same mistakes as despotic leaders did throughout history; plus, everyone deserves the benefit of the doubt. Both Emery and Everest are more hands-on so they supervise the operations of the orchard – both technical and research – and all things related to it. Val as the general accountant supervises all the other accountants (although I don't think she likes it very much but everyone has to take one for the team). While Gabe is a free thinker so he floats among the various business interests – whatever he is interested in at the moment. The spouses generally are in charge of supervising both the office and house staff. I have the mammoth task of governing, spear heading, the whole shebang. I make all the final decisions and sign off on all documents, give permits and permission for anything attached to the Whiley name. As a family, we make it work because of our commitment to the family name and our own individual legacy.

Chapter Two
The Origin of Emersyn

"Home is the place where, when you have to go there, they have to take you in."
– Robert Frost

Emersyn

Emersyn came into the Whiley family through a deal gone wrong. The most senior Whiley played poker with his most trusted associates who were all as crooked as they come. They each had great distrust for each other because of their many and varied sordid affairs (business and otherwise) that they were all involved in. In attendance, there was Rance Tillerman, Brady Madison, Frank Williams, Fred Mattison and Alton Little; all cotton farmers with some interests in distilled spirits. They were all in talks about going into the distillery business together, using their fallow land to plant purple grapes and talking to their congressman to garner support from the higher ups. However, that business enterprise was never meant to be.

On the fated night, that was as hot as a Texas wild fire, when tempers flared, they were all gathered at Adam's Bar and Diner in the back room where they drank raw moonshine and played antagonistic poker. On that august night, old Whiley was on a losing streak and was subjected to demeaning jokes and ridicule. Acram Whiley was as stubborn as the day is long and as the moon is constant. As a rule, he never admits defeat, which made him a great businessman but a horrible husband and poker player.

At that point in the game, he had lost his two most valuable horses, his strongest male slaves, his house and land. But somewhere in the back of his mind, Acram believed that if you stuck to it; ultimately, the god of perseverance would smile down on you – and this is exactly what happened. Whoever this god was and wherever he was, he did smile down at old Acram.

It is now a mystery to many how this game which had been stacked against Acram from the get go could take such a dramatic and drastic turn in his favour. In the middle of the onslaught, laughter and general tom foolery, when he only had his treasured twenty-four karat gold watch – a watch which had been won by his grandfather in a game, much like this one and had been Acram's father's as well – and the horse he rode in on, to bid with.

Suddenly, he had an excellent hand.

Witnesses said that the rest of the players had become complacent from their many wins. They each seemed to have all plotted and executed Acram's eminent defeat. Their tremendous smugness made them both arrogant and lax; hence, they missed copious opportunities. Subsequently, before they knew it, old Whiley was back in the game; full throttle.

Rance Tillerman, the oldest among them – a man who was equally stubborn and determined – came from a long line of wealthy slave owners and he had lived in Emersyn all his life. All his siblings had been there and it was their families' pride and joy – that was until Whiley acquired it in a card game – a game which should have ended hours ago – a fantastic showpiece, an emerald in the bushes. Fortunately, or unfortunately, his daddy was long dead but must have been turning in his grave. To this day, no one in Tillerman's family knew how it happened, the decisive moment; however, in the end when all was said and done. Tillerman had lost his home (where his entire family lived), the land it was on, his crops, his animals and all his slaves. His family's great treasure; misplaced.

Naturally, rumour had it that the loss was not as a result of the poker game but a business deal that went sour. Others said that it was to cover up of an even more sinister deed, still more sober minds said, it was the intoxicant. A few others said it was blackmail. At this point, who knows? But what was good and true is that the deed was done.

The deed for the Tillerman mansion and estate went to Acram Whiley.

By mid-afternoon the following day, Whiley, his wife Babs, their three kids and all they possessed had set up residence at Emersyn.

The slaves, collectively shook their head at the foolishness of the white man, agreed that it was a sign of his derangement and eccentrics. They really took little interest because their lives continued much the same, just more misery, more drudgery, disturbance and disruption. New owners who they had to impress all over again. Because, the truth is, they had come to see their lives as a form of sick entertainment for white folk who saw them as less than human but as pawn pieces; to be used by duplicitous men – who could literally sing their praises one day and could cut your throat the next. Also, how they saw it, is that, in this life nothing was theirs to have and to hold – as they could be sold or exchanged or gambled away at any given moment – so why waste time on emotional attachments. They were actually at the whim and fancy of despicable men who saw them as a little lower than animals; because of all, they were kind to their dogs, cats, horses and mules. Even their stupid chicken had far more standing than them. In any event, how could they see them as humans? Peradventure, if they did, they would be obligated to treat them accordingly; ergo, in order to maintain the business of slavery – slave holders by choice – had to hold dearly to the ideal that to be black meant an absence of humanness so they were created to be enslaved, to generate income for others. The quotation, *all men are created equal*, clearly did not apply to slaves. It just wasn't their human or constitutional right. Consequently, it was this narrative and the ensuing measures that kept slaves in their rightful place to preserve the status quo and maintain order. Sadly, their one constant was heartbreak and lots of it.

In the changeover between the Whileys and the Tillermans; in the commotion shrouded in hostility, they lost some slaves. The strongest and best vanished. That served to create even more acrimony and tension in an already volatile situation. Acram was of the view that, Rance had once again double-crossed him by stealing his slaves; while, Rance was enraged because he was of the view that he was an honourable man and did not appreciate anyone questioning his integrity – least of Acram himself. Tillerman strongly believed that Whiley had somehow concealed the slaves to initiate a feud between them and to justify his malice. To this day, the Whileys and the Tillermans are at odds. The younger ones are not even sure why at this point.

In the end, there was no proof either way, no one went to check because Rance felt like it was out of his hands, Acram was convinced that those slaves had been confiscated by Rance and a man convinced against his will is unconvinced still. Needless to say, the other land owners felt hard pressed to take aside some defending Rance's honour and some standing up for justice for Acram – who they felt had somehow been bamboozled. Nevertheless, in all of this, the people who suffered the most were the slaves – because in the absence of proof and trust – someone had to be penalised and they were the obvious choice, the sacrificial lamb.

Of necessity, life moves in leaps and bounds, so invariably the show must go on more or less as before on the plantation and with Emersyn, now the property of the Whiley family. For a while, they were the focus of gossip and many felt that for sure Acram would lose this property. In fact, there were wagers based on this fact.

"Only a matter of time. A leopard never loses his spot neither can a tiger loses his stripes."

But nope, it didn't happen! He probably would have except for his wife threatening to divorce him, take the kids and half of all he owns. Plus, the reality that, his colleagues on principle; even those who stood with him, would never play with him again. They reasoned that it was a myth that lightening did not strike the same place twice.

In the passage of time, life went on as customary and over the years, Emersyn experienced a lot of structural changes; except for her rich emerald colour, that never changed and also her foundation remains reliable, unyielding despite the passage of time. As it happens, Emersyn has become a landmark and a structural masterpiece, to this day. Emersyn is stately with: ten vast bedrooms, large windows and strong pillars (that hold her up, giving her both a majestic and fragile appearance). This embodies the design of the era in the Antebellum South. A rich emerald hue, quite unique at the time which has been well kept over the years; strong, solid wooden doors, which have been upgraded from time to time, the fire place – the centre piece – that has withstood the ravishes of time and the onslaught of family gatherings over the years.

She is deeply nestled among tall lush trees, surrounded by daylilies, daffodils, lantana, tulips, crocus and allium cernuum, all of varying colours; with the splendid mountain range in the distance. According to the *Biophilia Hypothesis*, humans always seek to connect with nature and other forms of life. There is always a mesmerising floral scent on the grounds of this spectacular space that hits you as soon as you clear the massive gates which hedge family in and kept others out.

Emersyn almost seems human at times; bright windows which do not only provide light and air – but also give the appearance of lovely, watchful eyes – a source of constant surveillance. Some of her windows have balconies which sing many love songs from past escapades and a few more modern additions, such as stained glass. Plus there are many frames and posts which function as her arms holding up her lavish frame; along with the inhabitants of the house in place. As a matter of fact, lore has it that once one moves into Emersyn, one will never be able to leave and or once one leaves, there is no returning to her hallowed walls. Some even believe that it is the spirit of the dead slaves that hold them hostage, as reprisal for their years of being held in captivity. Yet others postulate that no sane person would willingly remove themselves from the lap of luxury. Indeed, there is also the rumour that the spirits of slaves long dead still roam and haunt the halls of Emersyn. However, whatever it is; Emersyn for sure, keeps all her secrets.

Chapter Three
Sins of the Fathers

"Children have never been good at listening to their elders, but they have never failed to imitate them." – James Baldwin

Acram's Kids

Acram and his wife Babs had three children – two boys and a girl – in order of appearance; Luke, Faith and Lance. At the time when they made the move to Emersyn, the kids were five, four and two. Unfortunately, they were privy to the upheaval and bore the brunt of the ensuing trauma. A trauma which stuck with them throughout the years, clinging to them like an old skin that refuses to die. Their very existence was marred by this pivotal turn of events in their young lives. They were forbidden to romp with the Tillerman kids (Rance's grandkids) who were roughly the same age, who had previously been their playmates, in another life. But now that the tables had turned and they were now in a higher standing than the Tillermans, that congenial alliance had been broken.

All this was very confusing for all the children at first, why all of a sudden, they lived in a different house (a nicer and bigger house but still, it wasn't theirs), why the adults were always upset and why they couldn't play with each other anymore. It took the older kids a long while to adjust and ground themselves in their new environment, never quite sure where they fit anymore. As if by being abruptly and unexpectedly uprooted from their old way, they had somehow been thrown off balance, lost their footing and found it difficult to get up. It did not help that the adults were all too absorbed in their debacle to pay much attention to the emotional turmoil the children had been encountering. Why would they? Because isn't it a fact that children are resilient and their bounce back is quicker? True, but every child is different and adults tend to lump them all together and determine that what fits one must be beneficial to all. But that is not always the case. Some children are definitely more sensitive; hence, they interact with their environment in different ways. For instance, Luke seemed to thrive in his new environment while his siblings wilted.

Eventually, all the kids came to understand that something spectacular and life changing had transpired and they had to roll with the punches – as the grown-ups kept saying – so they did their best to adjust and keep pace with the new events that were unfolding. But life for them was forever changed and the trajectory of their life forever altered. They had to learn from a young age to both internalise and normalise change.

Needless to say, the Tillerman kids came to hate the Whiley kids just as much as the adults distrusted each other and the converse was also true. Not surprisingly, because the seeds of resentment and malice had been planted and nurtured while the kids were still young; their roots ran deep and bore much fruits; bitterness and unforgiveness being the most lucrative. Besides, it did not help that the kids were used as pawns in an adult game; thereby, teaching them from very early how to manipulate, sometimes being used as spies and messengers of hate. Especially Luke since he was the youngest. Apparently, the grown-ups; all be it farmers, had all forgotten about the natural law of sowing and reaping and that reaping is always more.

****

Faith

Faith, the second child and only girl was a temperamental child who was not really wanted by her parents, because her sudden arrival was as astonishing as a polar bear being left in their drive way. No, she was not a welcomed surprise. For starters, she came at an inconvenient time when relations between her parents was much strained as a result of her father's incessant gambling; an inconvenient truth that Babs had preferred not to deal with. Babs herself was a product of a similar situation where her father smoked, drank, gambled, lost often and was abusive as a consequence. He was a mean as a mother hen when he was drunk and she always felt vulnerable because she happened to have been born female. Therefore, she always prayed for male children because she felt like they got a better deal in the gene pool; meanwhile, girls got a raw deal.

By the same token, she was called Faith because Babs saw her untimely arrival as a true test of her faith. Notwithstanding, during this time period, boys were much preferred for economical and practical reasons; they could perform 'manly' work, perpetuate the family name and safeguard their business interests through brute force if it came to that. Certainly, from the get go life was never fair to Faith and she grew to be just a sliver of herself, always apologising, as if to apologise for her very existence. However, despite the emotional abuse, neglect or because of it, she grew into a very loving and caring young woman. She was always quick to help, self-sacrificing, without declaring martyrdom.

Always eager to please, as if always on the verge of saying, "Here I am, pick me!"

Seemingly, her inner child always wanted to recreate the parent/child relationship that she was deprived of as a child.

Inescapably, she was always passed over. She struggled to maintain friendships because she was so eager to please, to add value, that everyone in dire need would find her and after that need was met; they would disappear as quickly as they had appeared. Unfailingly, she broke her own heart, believing that each contrived relationship would last. Confident that each time would be different; of necessity, ignoring glaring red flags.

****

The Boys

Among the boys, in school, family grievances were played out in the school yard, manifesting itself in cuts and bruises. And of course, this enduring hate spread to other families as well; essentially, isn't that the nature of hate – it proliferates the atmosphere, contaminating everything it touches, much like a virus that is airborne? Hate is definitely not a thing that one must take likely. It is like a giant presenting as a baby and as soon as it is fed enough, it looms, larger than life. Consequentially, this deep sense of loathing started to manifest itself in other families, as it turned sister against sister, brother against brother and cousin against cousin.

Regrettably, there was no one astute enough to identify the ramifications of this hate. Everyone thought like a tropical storm, it would run out of wind and rain, not realising that it might have started off that way but with each family it touched, it grew bigger and inadvertently became an immense hurricane with astronomical gale force winds of pandemic proportions. Unfortunately, there was no Martin Luther King Jr at the time, to tell them that *'I have decided to stick with love. Hate is too great a burden to bear.'* And really, would they have listened?

Over time, some of the kids from the town moved away and were replaced by other kids who contracted the hate affliction. As part and parcel of the human condition, after a while, no one quite remembered the genesis of this ubiquitous unrest (not even the Whileys and the Tillermans). They held on to the sedimentary notion that something erroneous had prevailed which had not been ameliorated, not in the least. That being the case, generation after generation came and went, lived and died, experienced their own hardships, their struggles and soon the deeply entrenched hate was somewhat by the lapsing of time. Nevertheless, the two central families still did not fraternise; although their business dealings were analogous, well the older ones, who still embodied the scars of the discord.

Still, the residue of hate cleaved to them like a new bride, on her wedding night, clings to her husband. Also, whoever would become the head of the family had to be made aware of the dissension; per adventure, the same mistakes were made, which would not be prudent. Yet and still, the young people, were all expected to flourish and lead productive lives; notwithstanding, everything which had been hurled at them. Everything around them seemed to be transitioning monumentally but they were still moving in slow motion; technicolour instead of high definition.

Chapter Four
The Generations

"There is a mysterious cycle in human events. To some generations much is given. Of other generations much expected." – Franklin D. Roosevelt

The Boys

Luke and Lance, sons of Acram and Babs grew up amidst hate, manipulation and suspicion; hence, that's how they came to live their life. At school and later in bars, the boys could be counted on to get into fights. They swore like that's how they made a living. The problem was, based on the drama unfolding with their dad, he treated them more like buddies than his sons and they were constantly in collusion to '*one up Tillerman*'. Naturally, they lacked discipline. Lance and Luke had an inherent sense of entitlement. They felt like, not only did Emersyn and the land surrounding her belong to them, the entire community of Shrove was their stomping ground; therefore, they could take as much as they like without giving back. They came to believe that this was expected of them.

Unsurprising to anyone, Lance and Luke never learned self-discipline. They relished instant gratification instead – recklessly aggrandising their egos, putting innocent lives in jeopardy in the process. They had no filter and of such were like wildebeests roaming in the wilderness; except, Shrove was not the wild and the people not savages to be mishandled.

No one liked them much in those parts. No one had a kind word to say about '*dem Whiley boys*'. They were viewed with deep abhorrence and if Acram were hated tenfold, they were hated one hundred-fold. Decidedly, if they were belligerent to the people of their own social class, then they were immensely more diabolical and cruder towards the slaves. They were no respecter of person; boy, girl, lady, gent, old or young. Even as kids, they played dangerous games with the slaves and in adulthood, fathered many mixed children.

In fact, they were the first family to introduce a new race of people to their community. These mixed children were especially hated because of who their fathers were and because of a deep mistrust of the *other*. They were treated with the same disdain with which their fathers treated the slaves. This made these mixed children especially spiteful and dangerous, bearing no allegiance to none but themselves. These mongrels, as they were sometimes called by slaves and white folk alike were fiercely intelligent and very manipulative because of necessity, they needed those skills to survive. They were always in survival mode and always looking out for the machinations that would give them upward mobility.

Needless to say, Luke and Lance were the bane of Acram's very existence, always having to bail them out of one dalliance or the next. They always seemed to be on the prowl for trouble and certainly trouble would always meet them halfway; on his terms. Acram was at his wits end, in terms of a solution to his problem, at his age he felt that he had very few options. In his younger years, he would just bring them to the old barn and no one would leave until he had kicked some sense into them. But with a sigh, he had to admit that, that would have been too much for just him, if only he hadn't driven his own brothers out of town. He even contemplated shooting them himself like he would to any of his blemished animals (and for sure everyone in Shrove and the neighbouring communities would have turned a blind eye) but who would take over the business? Their half breed children? Absolutely not! He would set fire to everything before he allowed such a predicament to transpire. The irony is that, as much as Acram hated the fact of the existence of these children and as a consequence wanted to extinguish their fathers, it is the very fact of their existence that kept their fathers alive.

Moreover, even with Luke being the oldest, he was somehow more vulnerable to the plans and schemes of his younger brother. The general consensus around town was, *'Luke is an evil spawn but that one Lance is definitely an asshole! He's Acram's worse kid! In fact, for miles and miles, he is the worst kid in these parts!'*

Sherriff Armstrong never failed to remove his hat, scratch his head and solemnly declare, "Son of a bitch, Lance, is constantly starting somethin, with anyone. He doesn't much care who!"

For some inexplicable reason, Babs always got blamed!

31

Lance was always up to no good, a visual representation of the term bad seed. He was comparable to *Adam's evil spawn Cain*. The funny thing was, to look at him, one would not have known this. Lance was beautiful from the crown of his head to the very sole of his feet. He had inherited all his parents' most arresting features; certainly, the parts most well-favoured and thought fairest. One would think that Luke was the bad seed with his less admirable features, a crooked nose, deep dark eyes and a thick head of dark hair. But no, Lance held the prize for that, with his extraordinary looks, yellow hair and piercing green eyes.

He came to be the most feared and hated by their slaves. If Lance had been less arrogant, he would have listened to reason and gotten rid of all their children of the mixed variety but he wouldn't. Don't get it twisted, it wasn't out of any great love for them or their mothers, he got his kicks from seeing his image on many of their tanned faces. Despite Acram's pleas, he vehemently refused to give them up. By now, Babs thankfully had gone on to a better place so had been spared the shame that was her sons; especially. her most prized son.

Through divine intervention or maturity, no one knows for sure, Luke and Lance eventually got married and fathered legitimate children. Children who were hated by their siblings from the womb to the tomb. However, these marriages were tumultuous and abusive. One of the many repercussions of hate is that, one cannot project it externally without it being an intrinsic part of your existence. Yes, they both internalised and normalised hate and eventually they had to pay the price; especially Luke. Maybe, because he was the oldest; hence, held to a higher standard, but whatever, it was his time to suffer. Their years of unatoned sins had caught up to them and there was no Acram to rescue them, by then he too had moved on to greener pastures. He started to hate himself more and more each day. He drank more and started to feel unlovable. He pushed his wife, kids and even his beloved Lance away.

In the end, no one could have seen it coming. He and Sarah May had been married for five years and were about to have their third child; except that, that child was of a darker hue than his other siblings (pun fully intended). Yes, sweet, Sarah May had dipped into the cookie jar. Why shouldn't she, when there had already been a precedence set of what was permissive and the evidence glaring? Mixed children in a black and white world betray or bespoke of a certain comradery. No one knew who had sired this new baby. Certainly, their mixed *chilluns* were way too young themselves to father children. That really hit hard and Luke was beside himself with grief and rage. Luke was like an injured animal in his fury. In his wrath, he even tried to asphyxiate his wife but sounder minds prevailed. Next, he turned his attention to the poor defenceless infant before anyone could intervene and triumphed; because, no human can subdue an injured bear. Plus, who could have discerned the depths of his rancour towards a baby? There was no time allotted for anyone to have assessed Luke's state.

The sound of Sarah May's harrowing screams could be heard from miles around. She was beside herself with grief and Luke was still saturated in hate.

At the most opportune time, she left under the cover of night, along with her two surviving children and one of Luke's most reliable slaves. Luke never quite recovered from this. After that, he was never quite himself again; never the same. He became truly temperamental, thoroughly, self-absorbed and started conversing with himself. By all intense and purposes, he had lost all trust in humanity; not even his brother Lance could reach him. Judiciously, Lance had to take over the family business, it was the right thing to do.

On the other hand, while Luke smouldered in his pain, raging against his allotment in life, Lance thrived under the pressures of his new position. Early in his life, Lance had learned to charm and manipulate, to also spot an opportunity from miles away. Accordingly, this was his moment to shine and to thrive and absolutely nothing or no one was going to rob him of this moment. How many sons had the opportunity to reign while the heir was still alive? Not many! In fact, Luke manifested more than an inkling of the dark triad in both his personal and professional life; narcissism, Machiavellianism and psychopathy. A force of nature to be reckoned with, who never took no for an answer because all his life, he had been led to believe that there was always a way: you just have to be willing to shake things up a bit to find it. A very deadly combination but at the time no one knew anything about those anomalies. Everyone was just of the opinion that, this is just how Lance is, Acram's vile kid; he was a horrible child and an even worse adult.

Lance married his high school sweet heart, Nickosia – who was in every way a just a gem of a human being as she was willing to overlook his growing brood. In every practical sense, their business dealings were doing extremely well, their relationship was flourishing and their children thriving; this would have been more than enough enticement for appeasement. Despite all that, his demons would not be still. He seemed either unable to or to be more accurate, unwilling to even attempt to silence his baser needs.

In the face of all he had to lose; overtime, it was rumoured amongst the town's folk that Lance had set in motion a full out relationship with a beautiful slave girl named Lacy – knowing full damn well that wouldn't last, it couldn't last. How could it?

Nickosia, after much ringing of her hands and many days of deeply agonising thought, confronted her husband.

"Baby, I'm just going to come right out and ask you this, are you having an affair?"

He said, "Who told you that? Did that nigger girl tell you that? What else do you expect from a nigger? They lie all the time! They always lie!"

Nickosia insisted that she had not heard this from Lacy and added that she would never demean herself by asking her anything of the sort.

"You are my husband, the man who promised to love, honour and cherish me, in sickness and health; before all else."

He said, "Yes, of course! Have I not provided more than adequately for you and the boys? Look at this house that we live in, for Christ sake! You have servants at your disposal. So, why are you going to take the word of unimportant people above your husband who loves you; above all else?"

After which, he hugged her fiercely and assured her that, "Everything is fine! Why do you always insist on creating problems, where there is none? Why would you want to ruin our beautiful family? You know that I cannot let you do that, right! You mean too much to me! Plus, it's all in your mind!"

Nickosia was both stunned and stumped. She absolutely wanted to believe her husband but there was just something in her gut, gnawing at her, screaming, NO! HE IS LYING TO YOU! It was all so very frustrating for her and embarrassing for her family because she was actually Mayor Pittman's daughter so image meant everything to her family. Her mum and sister kept insisting that she leaves, just take the children and run; make a clean break, just like Sarah May. She was indeed tempted to; except that she both loved and feared her husband. While he was a gentle lover, great father and husband; the few times, he had allowed her to see him enraged, really frightened her. Whether or not that was his intention, she had learned her lesson well and she clearly did not want to be the one to piss him off; not now, not ever. Obviously, she knew of his proclivity for cruelty from high school. Notwithstanding, even his hug was strategic. She perceived that it was not just a benign caress but it was both a gentle reminder and an astute warning that things could get; well, tight for her.

A not so subtle indication that he has the upper hand and knew precisely how to wield it. That he had the ability to squeeze her to death and there was not much anyone could do about it.

Perforce, Nickosia decided to investigate for herself. There was just no other way Lance wouldn't tell her the truth, Luke was too far removed from the sphere of human involvement, Sarah May had left a few years prior (without as much as a goodbye) and Faith would never utter a bad word against Lance – neither would she defend Nickosia. Unavoidably, Faith lived in the same house but like Luke, lived in a different realm. A world away from Lance and all his shenanigans. She never ate with them and took all her meals in her room which was in the north wing while they occupied the south wing. This suited Lance just fine. He always claimed that his sister was *a whimpering do-gooder, a bleeding heart* – one he would not have bleeding away all the family money – *not if he had anything to do with it.* Needless to say, he has no place in his world for *her useless ass.*

Invariably, Nickosia perceived the trepidation in her when Lance was around.

That same evening when Lance said he was going to ride into town to meet with some of his associates, she decided to follow him on her horse from a distance. Nevertheless, instead of advancing north to head into town, he went south; to where the slaves were domiciled and intuitively that should have been enough; however, she had to complete her mission – see it through to the end.

Lance stopped outside, a well-built house (unlike the others) with a well-attended garden and a beautiful girl came rushing out. But what was more stunning than her beauty, was the fact that she was pregnant, which was quite obvious even from a great distance. As if that were not bad enough, what crushed her the most, was the fact that after Lance, *her* husband, dismounted from his horse he stroked the girl's tummy tenderly and all the time, his eyes never left her face; gazing at her lovingly. A look, she thought, was only reserved for her. It was all too much for her.

The whole thing was too deeply disturbing and it all became too overwhelming for her. Not surprisingly, she developed a nervous condition because she just couldn't unsee what she had seen. A woman knows. She couldn't think straight; she did not know what to do. She knew Lance well enough that he would discredit anything she said. He would find a way to make her feel like she was being foolish, going crazy. Shortly after the discovery, as if to reject everything that she had seen, she developed a fever; needless to say, her body was trying to purge itself – by any means necessary.

Nickosia is not even sure how she made it back to the house – no longer a home – too many lies. Everything from that moment on was a blur – faded, as if far away – possibly happening to someone else and not her. She kept asking herself, *Why me? When I've been a good girl all my life, always faithful! I've done everything right.* She even made Lance wait until their wedding night to have sex. But she was very quickly coming to the realisation that, because you are a good person, that was not enough to fend off all the darkness in this world.

In less than no time, her condition as quickly as it developed, got progressively worse. This stunned her doctor, because to him, it just came out of the blue. He prescribed what he could, medication for her body, not knowing that it was her heart that had been broken, her soul had been vanquished, which had the same effect of turning off the light upon leaving a room. She had been pushed passed the point of human endurance. Of such, treating an illness with the wrong medication is just as bad or maybe worse than not treating it at all. Not unexpectedly, this erroneous diagnosis only led to more adverse conditions.

So, her mind went away from her and voices took its place. In lucid moments, all she thought about was his betrayal. She couldn't put it out of her mind and the voices amplified her fears.

On one very unseasonably warm Autumn evening, when she could not seem to quiet all the voices in her head as they just kept getting louder and louder; more insidious, she jumped on her horse, like on another evening not too long ago. This time, she knew how to get to her final destination, she didn't need to accompany anyone. She rode her favourite horse to the slave sector, located the well-built house with the well-kept garden – mostly ruby red peppers, blood red tomatoes and radishes – knocked twice on the door and when Lacy lumbered to the door; as by now she was heavy with child, Nickosia shot her on the spot, four times. Maybe to symbolise the number of years she had been married to Lance – no one has been able to definitively say why. But her goal had been accomplished, poor Lacy was face down in a pool of her own blood so there was no chance of returning from this.

She had made a decision, a choice, now she had to see it through to the very end. Before, Nickosia had been at a crossroad, silently waiting for her life to improve, to get better, willing herself to be well, but being held captive in her own mind, now she hit a crescendo. No chance of a do over.

Lance, who had been alerted by his house slave of Nickosia's swift departure, followed her but as he approached, shot after shot rang out, disturbing the quiet dignity of the evening! He rode as fast as his horse could take him; unwittingly, he knew what awaited him. Needless to say, it was too late when he got there. Nickosia was just standing there with his gun in her hand. He approached her cautiously at first but then his arrogance got in the way so he couldn't see that a line had been drawn, a line he shouldn't cross. He slapped her once and she shot him twice. Then seeing all the blood and the bodies, she turned the gun on herself and the voices; forthwith went quiet, for the first time in four weeks. Sweet Nickosia was finally at peace. Lance, for the first time in his adult life, did not have a smirk on his face neither did he have a scheming thought in his head. He was as dead as a turkey at Thanksgiving. Dead at the hands of the gentlest soul he had ever met, the one who loved him the best. But imagine hurting the one who was sent to be your balm!

This left Faith, in charge of his three children, his business dealings and the beautiful Emersyn because Luke was far too preoccupied. Many declared that she would fail. After all, what did a woman know about business?

Chapter Five
The Ripple Effect

"A human being is a deciding being." – Viktor Frankl

The children were very young at the time of their parents' demise. However, it is very difficult to keep secrets in a small town – so by the time they were teenagers – they had been made woefully aware of the whole wretched liaison. This brought them shame and shame made them vile.

Many people in town felt that gentle, loving Faith was the most ideal candidate to raise these children. They felt that, she would be the one to break the cycle of the Whiley curse. Yes, after everything that had transpired over the years, the name Whiley had come to be associated with an accursed thing.

Faith tried her best to protect the kids, to guide them, to show them love. She showed more than an auntie affiliation towards them, more like a maternal inclination. Some believed that it is as a result of their ghastly propensities why she never married. As it turns out, some things are too deeply rooted to be repressed and or suppressed. That being the case, by the time the three boys Lance Jr (LJ), Lake and Lawrence were teenagers they had started to show signs of delinquency. These kids were approximately their dad's age when he moved into Emersyn – the event which triggered the whole debacle between their family and the Tillerman's. Be that as it may, in their late teens to early twenties, it was already apparent that their fate had been sealed in their parents' blood.

Without rhyme or reason, they started to get involved in petty crimes, then more serious ones; petty larceny, arson on a small scale and later assault. The sad truth was that they had the money and resources at their disposal; good old aunt Faith made sure they lacked nothing. They had everything that would make normal people content; but sadly, not them. There seemed to be a huge void in their souls and in order to fill that void, they were compelled to bring harm to others.

Against their will, they graduated high school and onto bigger crimes; assault and battery and murder. The three of them moved as one, they were inseparable. Therefore, to this day, no one knows with any certainty, who had pulled the trigger. In a time and place where there was no DNA evidence, their attorney was able to get them off on a technicality. He argued, how could three people all kill one person at the same time? Who exactly pulled the trigger? Who fired the fatal shot? These and all other such questions were left unanswered. The boys all had the same story and they were sticking to it. The Whileys were always introducing firsts in their small community. They were they first family to ever be tried for murder in their community. The powers that be had to fly in attorneys from out of state to try their case.

From the get go, this was a hard case to prove. As might be expected under the circumstances, money changed hands. Eventually, the boy got what amounts to a misdemeanour charge, a mere slap on the wrist. As a consequently, if the Whileys thought that they were hated before; after this case, they were despised more than the Grim Reaper. The young man who had been killed in the brawl was actually the great grandson of Rance Tillerman. Folks in the town were at their wits end with the Whiley men and would have gladly driven them out of town; but ultimately, money talks and criminals walk. They actually thought that the murder was some type of reprisal over the age-old feud between the families. But since nothing was concrete, there were no witnesses (who came forward) so nothing could be proven.

Surprisingly, the experience of being dragged through the judicial system and the court of public opinion; immensely, affected them and actually initiated a positive change in behaviour. But because all three of them moved like one entity, it is difficult to determined who was changed first.

As a matter of public knowledge, all three of them went away to fight in the American Civil War without being drafted. This was the first indication that these selfish rogues had changed for the better. All three were impacted by the war in different ways. LJ lost his right leg, Lake lost his right arm and the youngest Lawrence seemed to have lost his mind. Everyone unanimously agreed and they saw them as in some way culpable for a very young man losing his life. All that potential wholly eliminated from the landscape of human exploration. A young man who was kind and just and much beloved by his family and the community at large.

The Whiley boys seemed to have paid their dues and somehow being damaged during the war had paid the karma for the family. That seemed to have appeased the folk and Nemesis, the goddess of vengeance.

Life went on for them, as normal as it could have under the circumstances. The two older boys were able to settle down, get married and have children but Lawrence seemed to have lost his bearings. Lawrence's condition appeared to have worsened after his older siblings got married and had children. By then, slavery been abolished; hence, illegal. The brothers had to come together and decide on a plan of action, next steps, so to speak. Aunt Faith had died while they were at war so LJ was officially the head of the family business and therefore had veto powers. This was when he decided to invest in other projects, grow apples and peach – an orchard.

Once more, this sudden turn of events, pushed Lawrence further over the edge. The sudden changes of most of the slaves leaving, having to work with the mixed slaves (who look so much like him and his brothers), having to work in general, on top everything else that had happened to him in his young life, seemed to have had a more adverse effect on young Lawrence. Most of the mixed people who were previously slaves, determined that they were going to stay on and work with the Whileys.

At nights, Lawrence could be seen running around the periphery of grounds of Emersyn screaming incoherently.

When confronted by his siblings, he would vehemently state that, "Guys, I am protecting the border lands from the sphinx of darkness."

LJ asked, "What's that?"

Lake said, "How do you know he's there?"

Lawrence never failed to declare that, "Because, I am the chosen one!"

"Chosen one for what?" they both asked simultaneously.

But Lawrence never seemed to have an appropriate answer for that.

He simply stated, "Those who know, know!"

That always left his brothers scratching their head.

No one knew what to make of this. The older brothers tried their best to help him as much as possible. Be that as it may, at a time when so little was known about afflictions of the soul, there was precious little that could be done. They even assigned some of his responsibilities to some of the other workers on the farm. The first time this happened, Lawrence got into a huge fight with one of his half siblings – Laika.

Laika was probably one of the meanest, most ambitious, most miserable of all the mixed children and yet most beautiful. Most of the others were sympathetic towards Lawrence's brokenness; hence, would have walked away, but not Laika. Laika always had a chip on his shoulder and a point to prove. He was angry about the hand that life had dealt him and was always on the lookout for opportunities to change that and much like his father Lance, he could always spot an opening a mile away. However, LJ was also Lance's son, so he too could spot a manipulator a mile away. Therefore, LJ knew that Laika could not be trusted and would have gladly kicked him off the farm but at a time when labour was expensive and in short supply, he had to work with what was presented to him. Plus, Laika had long since proved his worth by being reliable and available; he always added value to every new situation, this also made him valuable to LJ; decidedly, this made LJ abhor him more.

Laika, could not be missed, not only because of his great booming voice and his height but also because of his striking looks. He was just as tall as LJ (who was the tallest of the Whiley boys, despite now having a limb) with beautiful tanned skin, blonde curls and dazzling green eyes. When he was a child, based on his many tantrums and sense of entitlement, he was known among the slaves as 'the beautiful devil' or 'the devil child'. Sometimes, even his own mother was afraid of him as he seemed to have been born with an intelligence, far beyond his years. At any rate, both LJ and Lake decided to keep a close eye on Laika; he just could not be trusted.

The older brothers tried their best to help Lawrence and to get him help but between the farm, their wives, their children, keeping up with the sweeping changes being implemented, they just didn't have the time or the energy to invest in him as much as they would like. Change, seemed to be Lawrence's trigger. If things remained more or less the same, he would be agreeable but the moment there was a need to do things differently, apply new practices and principles, occupy new roles, he would be beside himself. Plus, in their neck of the woods, there was no knowledge of mental illness and treatments, no knowledge of post-traumatic stress disorder; absolutely no knowledge of therapy for his condition.

One night, Lawrence was especially triggered and couldn't sleep so he was up to his usual shenanigans; running around Emersyn screaming. Each brother in turn tried to coax him back inside to the comfort of his bed. However, there is no rest for the weary so eventually they figured that he would tire himself out and in due course go to bed. This particular night triggered a new normal for

Lawrence. He started to march around the property both day and night and no amount of encouragement could get him to agree to give up his patrolling. He only passed to answer the calls of nature and for food. No one knew when or if he slept. As a result of the busyness of their lives, he was just left to his own devices, everyone agreed that that was best since he was not harming anyone.

Lawrence continued his nightly ritual for a few months. One morning when they woke up; Lawrence had disappeared. At first, they thought that he had just gone to handle his business but gradually as the day progressed, they realised that something was very wrong. His brothers paused the day's activities and along with the workers and the people from the town, formed search parties. They searched high and low, in neighbouring communities, they got search dogs. But to no avail. Lawrence had walked off their property and out of their lives. This had to be the answer. There was no sign of blood or that anything untoward had happened to him. The brothers were beside themselves with worry.

Immediately, the rumour mill started turning. Some believed that his brothers had grown tired of him and had him killed (after all, they had killed before). Of all the things that happened, this one hurt them the most. Some believed that he had been hauled off by some wild animal (possibly a bear) but there was no sign of that or maybe that sphinx he was yelling about finally got him. Others believed that he had been captured and tortured by the ex-slaves for all the pain and suffering at the hands of the Whileys. Still no evidence of this. A few believed that he had been captured by the spirits of slaves long dead because they wanted vengeance and rest. This held no water as it was an absolutely ludicrous idea. Eventually, people stopped searching for Lawrence and for answers and just chalked it up to yet another Whiley, being a Whiley.

Not his brothers though. They carried with them to their grave a combination of guilt and shame because of what they thought that they had allowed to happen to their baby brother. They often wondered if there was anything that they could have done differently. Lance Jr and Lake both lived to a ripe old age and saw their kids become adults. Lance had five kids (three boys and two girls). In order of appearance there was, Lance the second, Elias, Betty Lou, Sam and Leah. Lake had five boys, in order of appearance, Lake Jr, Aston, Mark, Fred and Lawrence Jr (in honour of his brother) but baby Lawrence died when he was two years old.

Chapter Six
A Twist of Fate

"She remembered who she was and the game changed." – Lalah Deliah

Faith

It has been a long-held point of view that women acquire *soft skills* from very early in life which overtime will make them effective leaders and these skills are fundamental to the human condition. These *soft skills* are communication, empathy and listening skills which are all essential for any success in interpersonal relationships and as leaders. Oftentimes, these necessary skills are lacking in male leaders but they are generally the preferred variety.

After Lance died, Faith was compelled by circumstances to take up the reigns as head of the family and raise his three boys. This was not always easy but she gathered strength that she never knew that she had. Lance Junior was an excellent leader but while they were at war Faith had to make sure that the day to day operations of their business enterprises went on as before. At first the slaves were rebellious; for one, Faith was a woman, and two previously she did not have much of a presence in their lives. But eventually she won them over through her kindness and compassion.

Under Faith's leadership, conditions were drastically different for the slaves. They got all their weekends off and an hour break for lunch every day. In fact, she encouraged a strong communal relationship among them and advised them to have a little garden to supplement what she gave them (which was not much as a result of the war). At first, the slaves thought that she was *playing* them (pulling a fast one), then they thought she had lost her bearing (much like Luke had). Eventually, they came to see her as the lonely white lady who was trying to befriend them. Ultimately, they came to see her as a very kind soul, who cared about their well-being, as she would ask about sick parents and children and even asked the one doctor in town to visit an entire family who had been smitten by unknown welts.

The doctor was at a loss but did the best he could because he was getting paid. At some point, everyone has to pick their battles and despite Faith's unorthodox practices, which were unprecedented on that side of the Atlantic, he still had to live. Plus, Faith's slaves were flourishing and everything was running smoothly despite the fact that the Whiley men were fighting in the war; therefore, the woman had to be doing something right. The doctor was willing to bet that she was on to something new and far reaching but being neither a gambling man nor a political enthusiast, he decided to let sleeping dogs lie. However, people in town had started to take note of what was happening at Emersyn, some decided to follow suit by giving their slaves Sundays off. That's as far as they would take it because after all, rules are rules.

Faith had no place in her world for these man-made rules. Rules that oppressed; having to contend with unveiled misogyny all her life. Naturally, she understood the oppression that the slaves faced and endeavoured never to bring harm to any of them or make her brothers' mistakes. She had taken out a new lease on life and was finally enjoying her freedom from patriarchy. Things ran smoothly at Emersyn during the war and business flourished. The slaves came to accept Faith's kindness and would do absolutely anything for her. She actually saw the slaves as human beings and they thrived under her tender gaze. Truth be told, they gave new meaning to going above and beyond. Therefore, Faith was able to supply other farmers with provisions that they couldn't grow because there were not enough young men to tend to them. Some of the stronger and younger slaves had been recruited for the war.

Miss Faith, as she was affectionately called by the slaves, formed a small committee of slave leaders, who reported to her, not on the missteps of the other slaves, but areas for improvement around the house and the farm. She listened to and implemented everything they said because as far as she was concerned they had far more experience doing this than her. They soon realised how much their opinions were valued and as consequence always acted in the best interest of the farm. Plus, Faith was not lazy; never lazy, always hands on. Much to the chagrin of the slaves (who felt an overwhelming desire to protect, the lonely, kind white lady) at times she could be found in the fields getting her hands dirty. This was indeed a novelty to the slaves, not even the white men got their hands dirty.

Also, Faith being a hopeless romantic, encouraged the slaves to get married. She invited the only minster in town to perform mass weddings. Now there was a novel idea, slaves encouraged to wed instead of shacking up. By the next year, there was a whole batch of little Faiths running around. This was very confusing for her nephews when they returned from war. However, they did not question their aunt's techniques as she had done a surprisingly great job holding things down while they were away. Who knew she had it in her?

By the time the war was over, and the slaves were freed, they were fully capable of running their own lives based on the guidance they had received from Faith. As it happened, after slavery was abolished, a few of them decided to stick around Emersyn for some time, before heading on to bigger cities in the north, where they had access to better jobs. As a matter of fact, all Faith's mixed nephews stayed on at the farm because, for the first time ever, a Whiley had treated them with the dignity they deserved. Laika who looked so much like Lance Jr was afforded preferential treatment and he thrived in his aunt's presence. Laika dreamt of the day that the news would come that his siblings had died at the hands of their enemies so that sweet aunt Faith would become his guardian. He watched everything that Faith did and learned from her how to lead, how to manage. However, empathy could not be taught so he came up short in this department. In his young days, he had been exposed to too much cruelty so his heart had been hardened. All he could visualise were opportunities for his growth and nothing else. As much as he loved his aunt, he would have gladly smothered her in her own bed if that meant advancement. If that meant, he could live in Emersyn and be in charge.

Unfortunately, for Laika, his siblings did not expire and pretty soon the war was over and they returned. Their return meant that things would change for him and not in a way that was beneficial for him as they would never see him as an equal. Unwittingly, Aunt Faith had given Laika a glimpse into what his life could potentially be and he thoroughly embraced it. In fact, the moment his siblings returned, he started plotting their destruction. He was just biding his time because deep in his heart, he knew that day would come. The day would come, when like Joseph, his siblings had to bow down and serve him.

Chapter Seven
The Angry Seed

"Indifference and neglect often do much more damage than outright dislike." –
J.K. Rowling

Laika

Ever since he was a child, Laika kept having a reoccurring dream, of a snake lifting him out of his bed, flying with him over the town of Shrove and then dropping him in a town that he had never seen before. This dream always left him feeling disoriented. He would try to describe this dream to his mum, Chai, but she was always indifferent towards him. In actuality, she seemed to strongly prefer her other kids who looked more like her. In one moment, she would sometimes stare at him for many hours then in the next pretend as if he wasn't there. He was almost invisible in his own house. This often confused him as a child but gradually as he got older, he started to understand why.

The only person who was perpetually kind to him was his aging grandmother, Mary. She was the one who always rescued him from his mum's angry hands. It seemed like she was always angry with him. She always had a radiant smile for her other kids; even his cousins, but none for him. Grandma Mary used to say,

"Girl, don't be unkind to this child! What happened to you was not his fault. He's as much a victim of that man as you were!"

My mum would always cry and say, "But, Mama, every time I look at him, it hurts! I don't want to hurt no more, mama!"

"Well, hurting your kin won't take away your pain, chili! He is your child, your flesh and blood, that will never change! He will always be a part of you! Men have the option to deny a chili, but us women don't got that option. The good Lord didn't see it fit to give us that option! Once a child come out of you, then he's yours forever."

The man living at his house was definitely not his dad as they looked nothing alike. In fact, no one in their small family looked like Laika. Also, while the man at his house never laid a finger on him, sometimes his words were far more cutting and Laika wished that he would just beat him, like Mama, and be done with it. None, of the other kids would play with him either, not even the other brown kids who looked like him. He would often ask his mum why but no answer would be forthcoming, she would just give him a blank stare. So many questions!

By the time Laika was ten, he had actually got some answers to his questions. For starters, the white man, who was the boss, who had hair and eyes like his was his dad. He didn't understand the dynamics at play here, but he knew for sure that him and some of the other kids who looked like him shared the same dad, but he seemed to look the most like this man. After this discovery, he harboured a dream, more like a fantasy of being rescued by his real dad. Although Laika was really shy – years of verbal and physical abuse had left him broken, he even developed a speech impediment at a young age. It took him years to get rid of this thorn in his flesh. Yet, fear and pain enabled him to build up the courage to speak to his dad one day. He was tired of his life, of being seen but not seen and definitely not heard.

Unfortunately, Laika's grandmother died suddenly. Mary just went to bed hearty and well one night and didn't bother to wake up the next day. In actual fact, it was Laika who found her dead that morning. He kept calling her name and shaking her but she wouldn't wake up and smile for him like she used to. This was his first close up look at the fragility of life. He discovered first hand, at a young age that you can literally be here today and gone tomorrow. Laika saw this as yet another attack against him personally, in a world that somehow took exception to his very existence. He grew even more reserved and resentful of his life. Who would rescue him now that grandma Mary was gone? She was more than just his grandmother; she was also his confidant. The one he shared his deepest secrets and darkest thoughts. The one who could and would always console him when times were harsh. Decidedly, now that his grandma was gone he would have to initiate steps to be rescued by his real dad – her untimely death left him no other option. The plain truth is, he was out of options, he was desperate and desperation made him restless. Laika's intense grief orchestrated a resolution for him. Of necessity, he would approach his father and explain his situation and for sure his dad would be kind to him and rescue him; primarily, when he saw first-hand how much they look alike.

Laika knew exactly when his dad would come around and where he would go – he would be visiting Miss Lacy's house; never mind that he had never visited Chai's house. Laika made sure he washed himself from head to toe and put on his Sunday best, so that he would look his very best for his dad. Naturally, being clean would somehow make him categorically more appealing and would make his dad fancy him more. Above all, he looks the most like his dad so thankfully he had that fact in his favour. On the big day, he packed whatever little possessions he had, wrapped them in a cloth, wrapped it around a stick and hid them in the bushes. Laika believed that his dad would take him away on his big horse, up to the huge house, where he would live out his days in peace and contentment and he would never have to deal with his mum's harshness or coldness ever again.

Lance entered the slave area to meet up with Lacy. He was in a foul mood and just wanted to be comforted by his chocolate delight. Then suddenly one of the mixed kids approached him. Instinctively, he discerned that this was one of his litter – a good looking kid with hair and eyes like his – a shame that he came out so dark. As he got down from his horse the boy was standing right in front of him. Whatever it was, Lance did not have the patience for it today. He was not a man well-known for being patient.

Little Laika approached cautiously, being so accustomed to being shunned and pushed aside. He had planned his whole speech in his head and recited it to himself many times, but somehow his words failed him at this crucial moment, everything was all smushed together. Plus, the thing about a speech impediment is that, it is always magnified under pressure. Instead of saying, 'Hi! My name is Laika,' like he had planned, he ended up saying, 'Hi, your name is Laika!' Nothing else would come out after that and might as well. What the heck had he just said to his dad, the most powerful man in the whole wide world? He just stood there looking at the man, the man who was his dad with mama's coldness.

His father asked, "What did you say, boy? What do you want, boy?"

Poor little Laika just stood there at the sound of his dad's booming voice. He looked about him and realised that he had inadvertently summoned a crowd. He was unprepared for an audience so to protect himself, his brain paused itself. He froze and his whole speech vanished from his brain. His dad stood there with a smirk on his face – a look that seemed out of place on such a beautiful face – demanding, 'What do you want from me, boy?' while mocking his speech impediment. This phrase had become more like a taunt than anything else. Laika started to feel himself getting smaller and smaller so he prayed vehemently that the Earth would open up and take him. But why would the Earth do that? Why would the Earth want him when clearly none of his parents wanted him?

He did the only thing that he could think of, he started to run and he heard his father behind him laughing at him. In truth and in fact, his father's laughter was so loud and infectious that everyone around joined in. From that day, that raucous laughing became the backdrop for many of his nightmares and daytime imagining. Indeed, any such hearty laughter would trigger him every time he heard someone laughing loudly. Naturally, he chose not to laugh at all; a smile here and there but never a good belly laugh. And why would he? Laughing is usually closely associated with happiness and joy and since Life afforded him with very few opportunities for mirth, so there was no plausible purpose for cheer in his world.

Laika had not known hate until that day. Sure, he knew apathy and resentment, but certainly not that expansive hate that was being exuding from his father; that somehow or other had tentacles that attached themselves to him. All the while, Laika kept asking himself, how could so much hate be wrapped up in so much beauty? That did not seem plausible. So many things did not make sense in his world. He wanted to ask someone but there was no one to ask. On that day, he was introduced to unfeigned hate. He hated his father with perfect hatred. A hate so strong that he decided that he would never attempt to see his father ever again.

The fact that everyone in his life had either rejected him or abandoned him, only served to drive him to himself. He found in himself a friend, why would he seek anyone or anything outside of himself. He learned to be self-serving and selfish ambition became his driving force.

Invariably, when he heard that his father had been killed by his own wife, he greatly rejoiced. He saw it as God, removing all his enemies from him and putting him in a position to be elevated. Yes, God was going *to make his enemies his footstool*. That was in his grandmother's Bible, so it had to be true.

Meeting his dad had been a defining moment for Laika, one he would not soon forget. That was the day, he discovered his true passion and purpose in life; to annihilate all the Whileys and take everything from them. He actually started plotting that same day. He grew into a moody man, a man who loved no one and was quite sure no one loved him. That was fine with him because love made one vulnerable so he was never ever going down that road again. By then, his mum and the man who lived at his house had died so he was on his own. He had long since given up on trying to create a relationship with any of his siblings (the black ones and the mixed ones). He felt that the mixed ones were way too angry, way too manipulative and the black ones though on the surface appeared to be docile; were not. His black siblings, though lacking in ambition, were fiercely intelligent and they seemingly could read him like a book.

Of necessity, Laika hated a lot of things and a lot of people but fundamentally, on principle, he hated people who could read his intention the most. Those people, he avoided like the plaque. That also meant that he hated his white siblings the most. Those he hated because they always pretended that he could never be one of them and the one LJ was just like him; scheming, manipulative, anti-social. Therefore, he stared clear of that one because he seemed just as dangerous as their father. Laika often wondered, how come he had so many siblings but was cosmically lonely and isolated.

****

I saw an opportunity when my brothers returned from the war damaged; especially, Lawrence. Lawrence was the youngest and most decent but decidedly I had to do what I had to do. I watched Lawrence for a while and waited for the most opportune time. Lawrence had made it easy for me by starting to wonder around at night in the dark screaming gibberish. All this tom foolery would have driven our father crazy. I resolved that I had to make Lawrence disappear and while my brothers were distracted by their grief I would execute my plot to take over.

On the night in question, everything went according to plan. It had rained briefly earlier in the evening and there wasn't a star in the sky; plus, the crescent moon kept hiding behind the clouds as if seeking comfort from the biting winds. Also, around these parts, the rain always seems to have a soothing effect, lolling everyone to sleep earlier than usual so there was no one out and about when I pounced, like an animal, lying in wait for its prey. More importantly, although crazed, Lawrence was easy to subdue because of my considerable height; plus, obviously he hadn't been eating for a while so he was a sack of skin and bones. I was almost tempted to scrap that plan and return to the drawing board; almost. However, I did not know when such a golden opportunity would be presented again so I had to go with it. More than anything else, Lawrence appeared so diminished that he might not have much longer to live.

Initially, I had only planned to make him disappear for a while, keep him hidden in the mountains but Lawrence was too paranoid and his paranoia made him dangerous. At the outset, he thought I was LJ but at the discovery that I was just plain old Laika, he became defensive. Regrettably, Lawrence had to be liquidated. I had no other choice if my plan were to succeed. I took no pleasure in doing that. Afterwards, I did something that I hadn't done in years. I wept bitterly. I tried to hold him in place but he kept moving around and I had to apply more pressure to immobilise him. I'm pretty sure his ribs shattered – there was a loud, popping sound like when we were kids and we used to throw corn grains in the bonfire and watch them roast – both his right and left shoulders were dislocated.

In the end, I saw it as a kindness as his fragile bones splintered easily and before you knew it he was hollering in pain. Plus, his life had become so meaningless and empty after the war. I told myself that I had to do it but that did very little to appease my conscience. When did I become capable of doing such a thing, inflicting so much pain on a poor defenceless, deranged boy? After the deed was done, I sat with him for a while holding him to my bosom much like a snake would cuddle its victim, crying over him, mourning his untimely death; then, I wrapped him in my jacket. I took his feeble frame to the mountain and buried him there. The mountain is always cool and peaceful. I figured it was as a well-suited burial place for him as any. He would always have the flora and fauna to keep his company while being close to home at the same time. I didn't have the strength to dig too deep though plus by the time I was done, dawn was on the horizon.

At first my brothers formed different search parties to look for Lawrence and of course I joined in but not to look for him. Why would I? I had come this far, there was no coming back from what I had done. My grandma always said, *if you make your bed hard then you would have to lie in it hard.* That is exactly what I had done; hence, my sole option was to lie in the hard bed that I had made. I purposely joined the search team where the sheriff was in charge. I was never far from him so I could plant a seed in his mind that quite possibly one of Lawrence's own brothers had offed him. However, I didn't start with the sheriff, I would nonchalantly insert myself in small group conversations and in a very concerned tone, I would state, 'He was a really good guy!' Invariably, people would join in singing his praises and I would be quick to add, 'A shame that he lost his bearings in the war!' People would be sympathetic, so at this point, I would offer, 'I hope his brothers didn't get tired of him and harm him!' There would be uncomfortable silence and my mission accomplished – because my point was not so much to convince them, but to leave an opening in their minds, that this might actually be a possibility – a reasonable perspective, I would move on to another group. By the end of the first week, I had created a buzz and a decent amount of reasonable doubt, I sat back and waited for the perfect moment to make my move.

That exact opportunity came sooner than I anticipated. Very early, on the Monday of the third week of searching, the great LJ, left Emersyn to locate me in my lowly shack to ascertain if I could give an eye on things.

He said, "I have to go into town to speak with the sheriff."

I asked a little too quickly, "Is there any news about Lawrence?"

LJ said, "No, but it seems like the sheriff has picked up a cockamamie idea that I somehow had something do with Lawrence's disappearance. You wouldn't happen to know anything about that, would you?"

He let that last part, *would you* hang in the air between us for a moment.

He gave me one of his piercing looks, that he was famous for. His eyes never leaving mine. I almost peed myself. Because that was the same exact look that my dad gave me the day when I wanted to talk to him. Those exact same green eyes, that set me on the path that I am now on and there is absolutely no recovering from. No going back from this. By share force of will, I held his gaze, green yes locked on green eyes, framed by the exact same colour blonde hair, only my dark skin separated us. We could literally be twins. But of course, good old LJ would never see it that way.

Anyways, he must have realised that he couldn't get me to betray myself so he said, "I'm going to need you to give an eye on things while Luke and I are in town!"

I said a little too quickly again, "Sure I can."

I had to tamper with it.

"I'll do anything I can to help!"

At that he very slowly drawled, "Help who, Laika?"

One thing with LJ, he almost never used my name, he always referred to me as 'boy', so anytime he used my name was for emphasis.

"Why help you guys?"

In a slightly feigned, offended tone, I added, "What did you think I meant?"

By then, he was already on his horse, his point already made.

Over his shoulder he tossed, as if in passing, "Do not forget your place, boy!"

But despite his attempt at being casual, I knew exactly what he meant. I know that he was issuing both a warning and a threat. I offered one of my widest, most convincing, stupidest smiles and drawled much like he did, withholding scorn, "No master!"

He rode away, yellow hair ablaze, leaving me in the dust that his stallion had stirred up in his wake.

After he left, I started to feel excessively nervous, like I when I was a child and had consumed too much of Mama's coffee, when I was warned repeatedly not to. Maybe I had gone too far. I seemed to have unwittingly awakened the monster that was my brother. What if LJ knew it was me who had planted that seed and worse, that I had killed Lawrence? How much did he know? But he could not have known. Who would have told him? '*A dead man tells no tale,*' that's what the man who lived at my mum's house used to say.

For the first time, since I concocted this plan, I started to have doubts. As much as I wanted to take my rightful place at Emersyn, LJ is not a man that I really wanted to tangle with; especially, about something as serious as murdering a brother and trying to frame another. But then, this is what I've waited my whole life for, how could I not see it through? I was starting to wish that I had not set this in motion. More than anything else, I was really starting to feel guilty about what I did to poor Lawrence. He did not deserve to die and be buried in a shallow grave at the base of the mountain. I started to sweat; suddenly, I wasn't feeling so well. What I'm I going to do now?

I decided to just go about my day as per usual, completing the task LJ had assigned me, supervising the work. Everyone knew what to do so I didn't need to do much. My presence was not really required so I know for sure that this is a test and as much as LJ had told me to *give an eye on things*, I knew that there was someone, somewhere giving an eye on me. This was a moment, I should have been enjoying, supervising my father's legacy but I couldn't. How could I? When I was definitely under a microscope. But who was watching?

Late in the afternoon, I just couldn't resist. I had to view Emersyn from the inside for what might be the last time. My aunt Faith used to let me visit her in the big office. I also know where they kept all the guns. I was starting to feel so anxious that I needed to protect myself. I did not like how I was feeling. After checking that the coast was clear, I slipped in through one of the huge back doors. I had memorised every inch of my father's house so I knew exactly where I intended to go. The women and children were upstairs taking a nap. So, I had to be in and out quickly and quietly. I grabbed the gun because surprisingly the safe was unlocked, which should have clued me in but I was way too anxious and wired.

Suddenly, there was a noise outside the door and in came tiny Tim, one of my half-brothers (one of the mixed ones, although he could be a cousin seeing as he's so small; no son of my dad's is ever this small).

He asked loudly, "What are you doing in here?"

"I could ask the very same thing!" I retorted defensively.

Tim said, "You answer first, seein that I asked first and you came in here first. Plus, why do you have LJ's gun?"

I got angry at that.

"Why do you assume that it is LJ's! It could just as easily belong to Lake."

I knew I was stalling and he knew I was stalling. We leered at each other for what seemed like an eternity. Then something changed in him, like suddenly he had made up his mind.

Tim said, "Look, Laika, I can't say I like you or anything and I'm sure you hate me but LJ has put a bounty on your head. So, everyone is watching your every move. He seems to believe that you had something to do with Lawrence's sudden disappearance. I don't even know why I'm telling you this, when you wouldn't have done it for me. I just can't seem to accept that you would hurt Lawrence."

He paused here, waiting for confirmation. When he saw that none was forthcoming, he continued.

"I know you had a few run-ins with Lawrence but there's no way you could harm a brother, RIGHT?"

So now we are *brothers*. That angered me. All the time I lived in isolation and no one cared. But now that little Tim, was desperately in need of answers, we are all *brothers*. What kind of fool does he take me for? Well, they all can go rot in the mountains, like Lawrence, for all I care. I don't need any of them. For years they've treated me like scum and now suddenly we are all *brothers*. Give me a break!

All of a sudden, my anger clarified my vision putting all the pieces together. I now knew without a shadow of a doubt that either way, LJ was going to find a way to kill me. He had somehow sniffed out the fact that I had killed Lawrence and while he couldn't prove it, it didn't much matter to him. He is a man who had grown accustomed to trusting his instincts and his instincts had placed me at the scene of the crime; with a weapon in my hand, so whatever happened I was dead meat for the crows. I had to get out of there. I had to run for my life.

I causally said to Timmy, "I did not do this!"

Not too vehemently to arouse suspicion. I had learned over the years that the guilty is always overly emphatic, they always had to prove themselves. Seeing that Tim was in a brotherly mood, I decided to play on that.

I said, "What reason would I have to kill Lawrence? He was halfway dead anyways!"

I could have kicked myself for saying that. A more astute person would have caught that, so I had to scram before Tim reported finding me here and our conversation to LJ. But how would I leave? Where would I go? I needed Tim's help after all.

I said, "Look, man, I had nothing to do with this, but it seems LJ has already made up his mind about this; his great grief has blinded him. He wants someone to pay and since, as you said, I've had run-ins with Lawrence, he wants to make me the scapegoat so I will need to get out of here!"

The simpleton actually said, "No, just stay and explain things to LJ!"

At that I laughed out loud, too loud, I almost scared myself and Tim actually winced. It was a sardonic, ugly laugh.

I said to him, "Well, give me a chance to go home and prepare myself before telling anyone so I can clear my head."

At this he actually smiled and shook his head, the fool actually thought that he had convinced me of something; although, I don't know what. At the sight of him, I remembered my childhood nightmare. Tim was the snake in my dream. I knew for sure that he could not be trusted. He saw this as an opportunity to endear himself to LJ. And why wouldn't he? I would have grabbed this opportunity myself. It seems like all of us were on a quest to find an opportunity in every situation. We were all my father's children, always being prudent.

He quickly said, "OK! But leave the gun here! I cannot let you take it! LJ would kill me."

Tim saw that my back was up against the wall and there was nowhere to run; therefore, he was lax and agreed far too quickly to allow me to leave. However,

I know that as soon as I turned my back, he would pounce, sinking his fang into me, like one of those snakes in mama's garden.

As per usual, my instinct kicked into overdrive, I saw an opening and while he was comforted by the knowledge that I would concede, that he, Tim had caused me to relent, I hit him hard on the side of his head with my father's gun and ran out of there like the devil was chasing me. The fool did not even see it coming. Just before he fell on his face, I saw a stupid, questioning look in his eyes; like why? I had no intentions of explaining anything to anyone, least of all a snake.

I didn't own a horse but that didn't stop me from taking one – one more thing added to my growing list of crimes against humanity – in these parts, a horse thief was the worst kind of scum. Yes, invariably, that's who I had become; the worst kind of scum. At this point and after all I had done to get here, it didn't much matter now, I had to leave. I had to leave the south and make my way north where rumour had it that things were better. No one harassed you because of your colour, there was freedom there. So that's what I did, that very moment, I decided that, that was where I was going.

When I get to the fork in the road which would either lead into town or out of town, I heard the sound of horses. I figured I would have been pursued but not this quickly. I hid in the bushes and prayed that my stolen horse would be quiet. Thankfully, he was. It was actually LJ and his men coming back from the sheriff's office. Clearly, that left me with approximately an hour (if I was lucky) to get out of there before he got home and found Tim unconscious in the study with a gun missing. He would not need to rouse Timmy to find out what had happened. One look at the situation and he would have summed it up more accurately than Tim could have described. As soon as the coast was clear, I made good my escape and something tells me; not a moment too soon.

I was now a wanted man, absolutely no coming back from this. There was no returning to Shrove or enchanting Emersyn after this. That being said, I know I will find a way to decimate the Whileys, taking all, they hold dear in the process. At this point, not even Lawrence's untimely death is near my conscience. He was the karmic selection for his family's iniquity; after all, doesn't every family have one? I most certainly am the oblation in my family.

Chapter Eight
To This Manner Born

"Life is a matter of choices and every choice you make, makes you." – John Maxwell

Mason

Mason is the great, great, great, great, great, great, grandson of Acram, who begot Lance, Lance begot Lance Jr, who begot Lance the third (who decided to change the Lance tradition) so he begot Adam along with two other sons, Adam begot Phoenix, who begot Yves, who begot Cahal and Cahal begot Mason. Cahal had been married to Beatrice for over fifty years and transitioned a few years ago. Beatrice has lived an exceptional life being the mistress of Emersyn which she never fails to share with any and everyone who would listen. Also, though she might disagree, she is quite eccentric. Secretly, she harbours a fantasy that she is Scarlett O'Hara from *Gone with The Wind* and Emersyn is her very own *Tara*.

Beatrice Whiley is the only child for her parents, Frank and Edna Godfrey. Frank was the mayor of his town from as far back as anyone can remember, even when he was on his deathbed the town's people refused to elect a new mayor. By small town standards that made them royalty. She grew up in a town smaller than Shrove; hence, a small-town girl, who was always treated like a debutant so came to expect that treatment as well. She also was and still is very narrow in her thinking as she had never been anywhere else but in the small part of the world and in her world, there were not many who were progressive in their thinking. The few who were more open-minded moved away as soon as the opportunity presented itself. Subsequently, she had nothing to compare her norms with and, how could she? Hence, she did not know that a great change was happening in the world outside of Shrove. Later she got married to Cahal Whiley, also very restricted in his thinking who had come to view himself as royalty as well. In every way that count, they were a good fit and they never failed to share that with their children. They would never publicly disagree with each other because that would suggest that they were not united and more than anything else presenting a united front, meant the world to Cahal and Beatrice Whiley. They were two people seemingly using the one brain. Cahal using the part that was great at business and Beatrice using the part that dealt with everything aesthetic. Naturally, Emersyn became even more ostentatious under her puritan flamboyance.

Mason is the first son among seven children. Of course, his role in the family is significant because it means that he has to carry on the long-held tradition of being master of Emersyn and everything and everyone connected to her. This is not always easy for Mason but he has had years of seeing his dad and mum take care of business, in a manner of speaking; so obviously, he has a frame of reference. However, lately he has had a deep longing, a yearning to do things his own way. He is married to Mauve and they have three children, Mason Jr, Marigold, Marla and their cat Chloe. Chloe is a Savannah Cat and she is quite small for her age and breed; consequently, she is always problematic, possibly because she has come to think of herself as human.

Chloe is like a child as a matter of fact. She throws tantrums and cries loudly if she does not have her way. For instance, if her meal is not done the way she likes it, she generally complains loudly to management. Chloe somehow knows that Mason is in charge and she never fails to convey her problems to him. Possibly, because he is always patient and kind, never yelling and always happy to greet her, which cannot be said of the other Whileys. She actively seeks out Mason to solve problems such as, a splinter on her paw or poop on her tail. There was that one time when Mason was in a board meeting in his office and her grievance was so loud, Mason had to leave and attend to her needs. He then had to coax her to get into a basin with water to wash poop from her back paws, but then she enjoyed the water so much that she did not want to leave. Most of the Whileys see her as a spoilt brat but they tolerate her, mostly because the kids adore her and look forward to her shenanigans.

Mason tries to live up to the expectations of his parents; unsurprisingly, he sometimes struggles because they are sometimes out of touch with the realities around them. For instance, they still wear the tell-tale manacles of slavery and colonialism through their insistence that Mason does not go into any business dealings with any person of colour. Mason tried to explain to his father first and now to his mum that, that is an outdated idea and therefore not how the world works anymore; that they now live in a modern society that embrace differences and use them to enhance their way of doing things; but they flatly refused to listen.

Subsequently, although they are not starving and never will, Mason believes that; overtime, he has missed many monumental business opportunities as a result of his parents' regressive ideas about maintaining the status quo; which is all this is. It confuses him also that for people who always emphasise the importance of being prudent, their whole way of thinking is so not prudent, at all. This is all aimed at maintaining control despite the fact that they claim to have handed over the business to him with so much fanfare that it was even in all the local papers. He does understand that they are a proud people who come from greatness – the irony being that they didn't always do everything by the book themselves – but just once he would like them to consider his inclination as it relates to running the business. The Whileys are famous around town for doing whatever they pleased, which makes it even more tenuous for him because what they have prescribed, goes against his very nature as a Whiley. Every Whiley likes to exercise autonomy over him or herself and find it tremendously tyrannical when they are asked to do otherwise. Sometimes the whole situation becomes so inordinately frustrating for him, that he wants to just hand over the reins to Emery, his younger sibling who is next in line to sit on the throne at Emersyn. However, he has long since arrived at the understanding that this is not how things work in his world. This would set off even the worst fireworks in his family and naturally he had absolutely no desire to do that. He much prefers goodwill and harmony among his siblings that makes for a better atmosphere in and around Emersyn.

****

This time around, I am particularly stressed because of a great idea that I have. There is an extremely successful businessman who has reached out to me by phone and video conferencing (seeing that Shrove is so far south) a few times and we have totally the same ideas and similar methodologies, we just mesh. He has great ideas about conserving the environment while at the same time, maximising the inherent potential in our land, which next to the people who work for us, is our most valuable resource. I've Googled him for my dad, had my guys do an investigation into his background and fact-check his theories. Yet, my daddy just wouldn't see reason and now that he has passed on, I've tried to reason with Mum but she won't budge. Each time she says, 'Mason, I will not dishonour your father's memory by all of a sudden agreeing to something that he would strongly disagree with!' Needless to say, there was a lot of yelling which brought everyone running. I wish Mama would see reason because I absolutely hate to fight with her. Two people in my life I hate to have confrontations with are my mum and wife; other people, I don't mind but not these two.

The problem is not the person that I want to go into business with, it is an inherent mistrust of anything, any ideas, any way of being that conflicts with their way of seeing the world that they are accustomed to. The guy is black so that's a huge deal for them. They believe everyone has his place just not a place in our business if you don't look like us and if you don't think like us because outside of that, there would be chaos. My daddy used to say, 'Mason, if it ain't broken; don't try to fix it!' I tried to explain to him in terms that he could identify with but no go! I told him, 'Dad, sometimes, the equipment on the farm and the computers aren't broken, right, but we have to give them a complete and thorough maintenance to keep them going. Right? We don't wait for them to break before we fix them. We keep looking for ways to improve our systems so that they can last.' At this he would nod in agreement. But then when I go on to say, 'So it is with our approach to business, sometimes we have to do a general clearing of our inventory, delete ideas that no longer serve us and upgrade our thinking to align with the current applications.' At this his green eyes would explode and I knew there would be a heated discussion for days and a general lack of mirth for a while – because if my daddy ain't happy, ain't nobody that's happy in this house. He would always declare mournfully, 'Mason, don't let me regret handing over my business to you in the first place. Your mama and I, are depending on you to continue the business and run it in such a way that we can be proud as you uphold our traditional family values.' I would always concede with a sigh, 'Yes sir!' Sometimes, I am almost tempted to yell, 'GET OUT OF THE 1920s! THOSE DAYS ARE GONE AND NEVER COMING BACK!'

In the face of that, I am getting older and I have a deep yearning to leave my mark on the world, leave a legacy behind which surpasses each and every single accomplishment of all the Whileys put together. My wife Mauve surmises that I am way too compliant to the whims of my family. She thinks that I should grow a spine and come out from under the shadow of my dad and his dad and the other Whiley men.

"Be your own man! Who is legally the boss here? You, sir! So, don't come whining to me about the wishes of your parents when legally you have the right to do as you see fit! Miss Beatrice is old and all her life she's been stuck here in Shrove, so what do you expect her to say?"

She keeps forgetting that one of my great, grandfathers (Phoenix Whiley) disowned his two sons because they would not comply with his wishes and it was on his death bed that he gave instructions to put Yves (his youngest of six children) in charge. These instructions came with a clearly, ratified and loophole free agreement that ensured that Yves walked the straight and narrow. Lore in the family has it that Yves was a very dispassionate young man who complained constantly; therefore, he did not mind things being so clearly defined for him, which also freed up his time, so he could partake in other activities that he revelled in. Also, the only reason Yves was put in charge was because, Phoenix wasn't going to put his legacy in the hands of women (he had four girls). Thanks to the team Great Grandpa Phoenix assembled before he passed, the business was kept afloat during, what is known in our family as the *Yves Years*. Yves could be careless about the family business; he was just happy to have access to resources to live a comfortable life. These Whileys are not to be played with and I wouldn't put it past my dad to have a fail-safe plan in place somewhere, in case I make a mockery of his name.

Nonetheless, Mauve does have a point, she always has a clear and specific point, but obviously she doesn't know my family really well. Besides, how can I do that and go against the undeniable wishes of my family which is so steeped in tradition; especially, when there is a specified path for me to take? For this reason, my mum believes that I should have never married that girl, with her opinions and new ways of thinking. She believes that I should have married a girl who is more in keeping with the values of our family (by this she means, her values). The choice of who I marry was one choice that I would not allow my family to make for me. Mauve also wants me to threaten my mum. *If you don't allow me to do as I please, I will quit and move away!* But at my mum's age, I could never say that to her and I would never do that either. Mauve has given up on me and now her only solution is: 'Well, continue to suffer in silence then!' I hate when she says that. Some things are easy for her to say because of her family and her experiences.

Mauve was born in the south but she went north for school, so she has brought back a lot of liberal ideas about how the world should work. Also, through her studies, she has crossed paths with a number of different people; of different races and places, so she is of the view that people are people. Nothing else matters. Again, easy for her to say.

Sometimes I do feel like I am stifling and it's hard to communicate, even with my siblings. For one, there's a split in how we should proceed, half my siblings agree with my parents (the older ones) but the younger ones are diametrically opposed to their archaic ideas. This sometimes made for very interesting dinner conversations. One thing that is good and true about the Whileys is that, we all have an opinion about everything and we are unafraid of expressing said opinions simultaneously. It is in times like these that I am happy that at least I am in charge and I have veto powers to shut down these conversations when they become too spirited.

In all honesty, my position as a monarch means that I should try not to exercise any kind of favouritism or entertain the idea of favourites. That being said, if I were pressed to nominate one; it would have to be Valencia. She is the most level headed, intelligent, compassionate of all of us and certainly of anyone that I have ever met. A self-proclaimed empath who protects her energy by not allowing herself to become *unhinged by any of the events in this house* (her words).

On a particularly emotionally exhausting day when the complexity of my decision or a lack thereof weighed too heavily upon me; late in the evening before supper, I decided to go for a walk around the grounds – as Emersyn's natural beauty sometimes provides a balm to pacify the quandary in my mind. I saw Valencia (Val as we fondly call her) sitting under an old, over grown poplar tree. The tree is so old that her roots can be seen all around her, the branches are so full that they look like nests from a distance and despite the coolness of the evening, offered a certain warmth that is sometimes unexpected. This tree with her alternating, oval and heart shaped leaves, has been around for so long that as children we named it Buddy. Many times, we would hide in her branches during a game of hide and seek or to hide tears brought on by heart break. So, on this very perplexing day, I decide to join her – not to commune with her but just to sit quietly – just be still, as stillness sometimes is very soothing for me. Also, I know that at times like these Val likes to just luxuriate in the serenity of the moment.

Without intending to, I somehow disturbed her sense of peace. At my approach she seemed startled and looked at me as if I had scorched her. She raised familiar green eyes to my face and must have seen the strain there. She observed this.

"Why so hampered with such a heavy load, big bro?"

She does this sometimes, identify with my 'load' as she calls it.

****

I said, "Well, you have knowledge of the situation that I am wrestling with. I am at a crossroad and am unsure how to proceed, that certainly has not changed!"

She said, "You mean, you do not want to hurt Mama because fundamentally, that is the issue here. Because you already know with your head that you are in charge but it is your heart that is indecisive. But as you know, the Bible says, *two cannot walk unless they be agreed* and it seems like your head and your heart are the two that need to come into agreement. It is not Mama you are fighting with, it is yourself. Eventually, Mama will come to accept whatever decisions you make and you have to choose for yourself to show her that you can, to show her that you will take initiative when it counts and that you won't always look to her or anyone else for counsel."

I wanted to react to that but I could see that she was not done. She continued, "You also have to make it plain to all of us that you are in charge now, not Mama or Dad. The truth is, Mum is on her way out so she is rooting for you to make good, carry on the family name and build a legacy for yourself and your son who will someday take over the family business. So, what are you afraid of? Why are you afraid to move in the direction that your heart seems to be taking you in? Are you afraid that your greatness will outshine all the Whileys before you? Because if that is the case, that is fine. The Whileys expect greatness from their descendants, it is not only expected but encouraged. Are you worried about failure? Because that is fine too. Failure will take you where you need to go not just where you intend to go."

"For someone who is a self-proclaimed introvert, you certainly have a lot of words today."

At this, we both laugh. I sit next to her and gently take her hand. I don't know why. I don't usually do this. I guess that with everything I am feeling particularly vulnerable today.

"Thanks, that's actually great advice! Who knew you were this smart?"

We laugh again.

"I know what is expected and I want to do that, believe me, I do. But although this is the right decision, there's something inside me telling me that there will be no coming back from this decision. I feel like I am taking a path that none of the Whiley men have ever taken before and it has the potential to disrupt the natural order of things forever. I am about to make a decision that will forever change who we are as a people and of such there will be no take backs, no do overs. Whatever it is, I am going to have to stand up to the consequences and face my fears. To your point, I am not afraid of making a blunder, I have been in business for a long time and I have watched Dad in his business dealings to know that failure is not the end neither will it define me. However, I am just afraid because I feel like, I am about to cross over."

"Cross over? What does that mean, Mason?"

"I'm not even sure myself but that's the most appropriate term that I can think of to describe how I'm feeling right now."

I sigh and she gently squeezes my hand, encouraging me to go on, reassuring me that I am safe with her. I continue,

"Remember, when we were kids and Dad used to take us fishing?"

She nodded, just like when she was a kid and Mum gave her an instruction.

"Well, he used to take us to the place where the trees form an arch next to the river and told us that, at that place, we should never cross over because once we do that, we're going to be on someone else's property. Remember, how he used to stress the significance of knowing where the boundaries are and staying within ours? And most importantly that we should never allow anyone to erase our boundary or take our land! Well, that's what I mean. I feel like I'm about to cross over."

Val's turn to sigh.

"Well, even if that is so. The fact that your gut instincts are propelling you to act, then that simply means that this is something that was ordained to happen, *from the foundation of the world*, it was meant to happen. So, the problem you're experiencing is the fact that you are fighting against fate, against your destiny, against yourself even. And that's why this is so tremendously taxing for you because this is something that has been predestined; hence, it goes beyond you and the Whileys. Thus, this needs to be done."

We sit in silence for a while, enjoying the stillness of the moment. It feels like time is standing still and even the wind holds her breath. The leaves are motionless as if they are anxiously awaiting what I would say. The little bit of daylight left now seems like a spark to underscore the significance of the moment. And just like that, I knew what I had to do. We sit for a few more minutes to let the gravity of the moment marinate in the stillness not knowing when such a moment would come again.

Then we heard the bell toll, summoning all the Whileys to supper, as is our custom to break bread together every day (at least once per day).

That night, I made passionate love to my wife (for the first time in a long while) and then I had one of the most restful sleeps I have had in years. I even had one of the finest dreams I've had in a long time. I dreamt that I was standing on my balcony, looking across at our orchard and it was the biggest harvest we had ever seen. Each and every tree was laden with beautiful ripe apples; remarkably, like a colourful canopy apple covered every inch of the grounds of our orchard as far as the eyes could see. There were no bad apples (for lack of a more apt term) they were all rich in colour, ripe to perfection and in varying shades of red, pink and green. I could even smell their rich sweetness from all the way up here. As I looked more closely, I realised that intertwined among the apple trees were rose trees of differing variety and they were all in bloom, pink, white, red and even yellow. It is the most glorious dream that I can ever remember having.

This dream and the overall feeling of well-being that I woke up with, just reinforced the fact that I was doing the right thing, on the right path. I even had a pep in my step, a tune on my lips.

Mauve even remarked, "You're in a good mood, sir!"

"Yes, I sure am."

"Do you care to share the source of your sudden zest for life because all day yesterday, every time I saw you, you were just moping around the house, now look at you as chipper as a bug on cake."

We both laughed and I know I did well last night because she has not laughed like that in ages.

"Did you meet an oracle in the bushes yesterday? I saw you going out to visit Buddy yesterday in the evening. I was going to join you but honestly, I couldn't be bothered with your brooding. Good old Buddy must have imparted some words of wisdom to you."

I told her that I was working through the details and I would let her know soon.

She said, "As long as you're OK, then we're OK, so I'm OK!"

Music to my ears.

I had a plan and nothing or no one was going to change my mind. I went to check on Mum to see how she was doing. Of course, Chloe went with me. Mama hates Chloe. In the middle of complaining about ankle pain, knee pain, back aches, Chloe kept touching her on her ankle with her right paw. I told her to stop and she just looked at me with her green eyes. Mama never liked animals and we were never allowed pets as children but I decided that I was not going to rob my kids of such an important part of their childhood. The problem is, Chloe never listens to Mama. She listens to Marla (our youngest) and everyone except for Mama. Also, Chloe was famous for pouncing on Mama's food tray (again, Mama is the only person who would subject to this abuse). Maybe somehow, she knows that Mama couldn't move as fast as everyone else.

Lately, Mama developed an appetite for white rice and at the same time Chloe did as well. The problem is every time Chloe had rice she would be sick for days. We all figured that Mama was entering her second childhood because despite knowing the adverse effects rice have on Chloe, Mama would repeatedly feed it to her. Mauve was at her wits end with both Mama and Chloe. Needless to say, by the time I made a hasty retreat Mama was yelling, 'Damn you, Chloe! I hope you choke on white rice!' Chloe managed to make quick recoil before being hit by mama's breakfast tray. When we were safely outside, I attempted to reprimand Chloe for the hundredth time. She just meowed and walked away with her tail in the air, as if to say, 'mission accomplished'. Effectively, Chloe has successfully ruined Mama's day. Her gait indicates that she had gone on an undertaking and had been declared unanimously the winner. I couldn't help but declare aloud, 'Gotta love Chloe's confidence.' Mama was still in her room yelling, 'Damn that cat!' I need to develop Chloe's level of confidence as well, just do what I need to do regardless of the consequences and not be hampered by fear of making others angry.

By the time Chloe had disappeared around the corner, meowing happily, I was already dialling a number that had been previously taboo.

Chapter Nine
A New Life

"Don't grieve. Anything you lose comes round in another form." – Rumi

Laika

After Laika was forced to flee Emersyn, life was very difficult for a while and he desperately missed the routine of home. He started to believe that he would never be able to put down roots anywhere. Laika ended up doing a lot of odd jobs here and there that he had no passion for and being proud and arrogant did not help. He could never banish the idea from his head that he was the son of Lance Whiley so his life should be one of ease and simplicity.

However, the one thing Laika had which set him apart from many others was his ability to learn, assimilate and adjust. Growing up in the family that he did; unwittingly, had given him the life skills he needed to survive. Also, his striking blonde hair, brilliant green eyes, his height and sonorous voice which could be heard; seemingly, from miles around, just could not be overlooked or dismissed. As a matter of fact, he had made that a life goal, to never be dismissed or overlooked again. He soon recognised that among the recently freed slaves and people who had always been free were a sub-group; the brown aristocracy – people who looked exactly like him – but had money and were unwilling to share it with just any one. Never, in his life did he ever allow himself to believe that there are people in the world who looked like him and were progressing without Lance, LJ, Aunt Faith or Emersyn. At first, he was mesmerised by the very idea; that he, Laika, could make something of himself without the backing of his father's wealth. Why should he not be able to when people around him who look so much like him could? Laika carefully considered his options and decided how to proceed because he knew that working like a slave was definitely not his forte. He was born into wealth, though none of it belonged to him but very soon, he could make some wealth for himself. He started to nurse another dream, of returning to Emersyn with his wealth, new clothes and air of an aristocrat just to see the look on his brothers' faces; primarily, LJ, the very bane of his existence.

With this new knowledge, he just had to figure out a way to get close enough to this money so he could get some. He soon targeted the family that lived on the outskirts of town, in the biggest house in that area (mind you, not as huge as Emersyn) he always found a way to compare everything to Emersyn. He soon noticed that there was a beautiful black girl (Avant that was her name) working there and he decided to befriend her. After watching her every move for a while, he accidentally pumped into her in town. The poor girl was smitten, for her it was love at first sight, and although Laika lacked social skills, that much was clear. Being the person that he was, he soon found a way to use this to his advantage. He probed her on the inhabitants of the house and soon realised that in this family of means, who belong to high society, there was a girl with skin like his of marrying age and he suddenly realised that was going to be his way in. His way into this new life, a life that he had craved all his life. But he did not allow himself a chance to hope; per adventure, his hoping would be in vain.

Laika continued to 'see' Avant and sometimes she would sneak him into the house. During those moments, he would observe very carefully the things that the people in the house valued the most. He discovered that the dad was a farmer who had inherited money from his white mother who had died when he was really young but had enough sense to leave him a heritance. He was married to a brown skin lady as well and the union had produced two girls (no male heirs) Laika thought that for sure Mother Nature was on his side.

Laika decided that he was going to have to work really hard to impress these people and a part of impressing them relied heavily on his ability to create a very credible story about his origin. After staking out the town for a few days, to see what his options were, he decided to get a job with a tailor (he knew nothing about that job) but he was able to convince the tailor that he was a fast learner. The tailor decided that with Laika's natural good looks and physique he would be able to attract good business. The tailor, Mr Burnam, had no children; hence, no heirs. He had dedicated his whole life to his craft and did not have the personality nor the means to attract a wife. Again, this proved favourable for Laika who could be as charming and gracious as a politician whenever the occasion called for it. Naturally, Laika and Mr Burnam were a good fit, two very lonely people in a harsh world and Laika was desperately in need of a father figure (although he would never admit to this). They hit it off right away and pretty soon, Laika had unveiled a new business plan to attract customers to Burnam's lowly establishment. Effectively, Burnam, without intending to, became a father figure for Laika.

Laika was quite business savvy, he worked hard and after a while as a result of his sound business sense they were the most sought-after tailoring establishment in town and for miles. Laika was able to establish contacts (having watched the Whileys accomplish this, it came as second nature to him) with merchants who came through town and was able to purchase fabric at a wholesale price in exchange for setting up a place in the store to sell their fabric; at a cost. Therefore, ensuring that they had access to the best fabric at a reasonable price. Also, Laika collected commission on each piece of fabric sold. This worked quite well for Laika and through conversations with these merchants who had travelled all over the country, he was also able to design suits that previously had never been seen in the north before. In addition to that, another part of their business plan was to have Laika wear the suits that he had designed around town because surely with his height and natural good looks Laika could not be missed. The business became so lucrative that they had to purchase a bigger building to house the fabric, the finished products, the work area and of course Laika's office. Laika also became the chief trainer for all the new employees, he just did not want them learning any bad habits from Burnam who was too laid back. Burnam clearly lacked Laika's drive and desire to succeed.

Laika was indeed an overnight sensation, a big hit in town. Pretty soon no one could remember a time when the tall, dark and handsome man, with the bright blonde hair and brilliant green eyes had not lived in town. No one knew where he came from and no one cared. Laika was making enough money, had enough resources to do whatever he desired for the first time in his life. For the first time in his life, he could actually exercise autonomy over his life. Laika started to get invitations to the most lavish and exclusive parties in town. He rubbed shoulders with the mayor, the judge, rich business men (black, white and mixed) and the crème de la crème. But none of that brought him the satisfaction he craved because this town was not Shrove, he was not living in Emersyn, his ultimate dream and did not have his siblings around to witness his success.

Over the years, he had decided that he no longer needed Avant and surmised that she might be a liability to his plans seeing that she had known him intimately. Therefore, he decided that she had to be eliminated seeing that she was the only one in town who could ruin his plan. When the business had taken off, Laika had suggested a few times that maybe, just maybe they should tell people that he was Burnam's nephew, to create the feel of a family run business. Burnam happily ran with this idea as he was of the view that this was his original idea. That's the other skill that Laika possessed, he could easily convince people that *his* idea was all of a sudden, *their* idea. After some time had passed, the town's people genuinely accepted Laika seeing that he was the old man's long-lost nephew, who had suddenly appeared in his life and brought with him the wind of change that had brought success to not only Burnam, but the town as well. Suddenly, people from neighbouring communities and miles around started coming into town to purchase suits and fabric and while they were there they would patronise other establishments as well. Naturally, this was a plus for the town and no one could dispute the fact that Laika had a huge role to play in this new economic upturn in their town.

Laika's plan was going well as he soon got an invitation to dinner from the people who lived in the big beautiful house just outside of town, that was not Emersyn. When he got there, he saw Avant and right then and there he decided that she had to be convinced to leave town, one way or the next, before he activated his plan. Plus, she was being way too familiar, not at all befitting her station or his. Laika was sure not to make any promises to Avant but over the years, she had gotten the idea stuck in her head that someday, they would marry and somehow live in this big, beautiful house together and raise beautiful children here as well. But one thing Avant had not counted on was the fact that Laika was not about to share his dream with her. For starters, she was way too dark and that would not be good for the children, neither would it be advantageous for the image Laika was trying to create. Ultimately, Avant had to go and that was a fact of life because Laika could not see any other way around the situation as she was the only person in his new life who could ruin all he had worked for. Sure, he knew she loved him or he thought she did, or he thought that she thought that she did. But years ago, he had decided to never give into the sentimentally that is attached to love, the idea of love because really in his world he had no place for love; what did love have to do with it anyway? You just do what you have to, to survive. Love will always slow you down, so no, a thousand times no, he had no place in his heart or his world for anything remotely resembling love. He hadn't been brought up with love, he needed it when he was little but didn't get it, so surely now that he was grown, he did not have any further need of it. It was a luxury that he could easily live without for the rest of his life.

After work the next day, just like in another life, he met up with Avant and encouraged her that they needed to spend some time alone, away from the maddening crowd as his new life had made him a celebrity in town. Everywhere he went everyone knew Laika, even the children and you know that you are famous when even children know your name. As usual, Laika used his power of suggestion to convince her that they should go for a walk in the remote area that was close to the town. Of course, Avant thought that this was such a romantic idea; especially, since Laika had even packed a picnic basket. She was thrilled to bits to go with him and why would she not trust him to act in her best interest? She had known him for a while, he was a very successful man and a local celebrity in town. Ironically, these are the exact reasons why she should not have trusted him.

At the designated spot, they set up their cosy spot (Laika thought of everything) a large plastic bag to prevent the ants from crawling onto their food and a huge blanket for them to rest or recline on. Things were going well, pretty well actually until Laika suggested that Avant left town. At first, she assumed that he wanted to elope with her but soon discovered his full meaning and the weight of it was quite crushing for her. He did not want her, never did.

Initially she questioned, "Why would you want us to leave now when you're doing so well?"

He flatly stated, "Not me, just you."

Seeing the look of disappointment on her face quickly added, "Not me, or we, just you. Just for now! Just for a short time."

But she continued to question his intentions, his motives and Laika could not stand to be tested. Suddenly, he dropped his veneer of charm and air of congeniality and what she saw was a completely different Laika. That was the last thing she ever saw.

Avant did not see it coming so she did not even think to run or scream and this far out in the boonies what would be the point? Who would hear? The last thing she saw, apart from his yellow curls that looked viperous and the venom in his eyes, were his hands reaching for her throat and wrapping around her like an angry python and squeezing the very life out of her. Avant never saw this coming, never saw such murderous tendency in such a beautiful man. How sad is it that so much beauty could be wrapped up in so much hate and bitterness? The last memory she had was the love of her life, taking her life.

Having efficiently accomplished his mission, Laika wrapped Avant in the blanket, along with all the evidence of the picnic and then the plastic and buried her at the foot of the hill in a shallow grave; much like he had done many years prior. But there were no tears; not this time, no loving embrace; just a job that needed to be executed with speed and accuracy. Then, he was on his way, to claim his new life and a new bride because the truth about Laika is, once he had set his affection on a thing, a person or a course of action, he had to see it through to the very end.

He went back to his new home that he had recently purchased (nothing too fancy because he had set his attention on another house) had a shower, a glass of chardonnay and went to sleep. He wanted to be fully rested as tomorrow would be a big day for him. And just like that, he put Avant out of his mind – out of sight, out of mind – that had become one of his new sayings. It's funny how he could get neither Emersyn or the Whileys out of his mind.

Early the next day, he was up, did his work out, had his coffee, mused on how much his life had changed and how well he was doing, all the while thinking that Lance would have been so proud of him. Laika had arranged for Burnam to meet him at the beautiful house and then they would enter together (just an uncle speaking on behalf of his nephew). Burnam, would actually be putting forward a proposal for Laika and the beautiful Mary Ann to be wed. Things had to be done the proper way and this was the way Laika had envisioned things being done.

Mr and Mrs Wilburn and Beryl Cardinal, Mary Ann's parents, who lived in the beautiful house were quite thrilled with the idea. After all, Burnam and his lovely nephew had made quite an impression on them and indeed the whole town. They had made a name for themselves and had created a legacy as well that would last for generations. So yes, they loved the idea of sweet Mary Ann being married to this beautiful young man but the only problem was their name. Seeing that they did not have any sons, their name would not live on, so instead of Mary Ann taking his surname, their only request was that he took theirs. That was quite an unusual request, one that neither Burnam nor Laika was prepared for but in true Whiley style, Laika could already see the advantage in that. That would mean, he would be the heir apparent (just like LJ). However, in a bid to not reveal his hand or his thoughts and to not appear too eager because that would

73

spell desperation, he agreed to consider the matter over night and then return the next day with his answer. Clearly, he had already made up his mind because really, what's in a name? A rose apple by any other name is just as tart. Plus, he had borne the name of his maternal grandmother for years, not his father's; therefore, he had no great attachment to said name. As a matter of fact, he very rarely used that name. When introduced, he would just provide his Christian name and not his surname. Definitely no love loss there and he could gladly part with a name that bore no authority which gave him no power.

However, Cardinal was a different matter altogether. Indeed that name sounded so regal, so dignified and so distinguished. He tried it a few times and loved the taste of it on his tongue and the smell of it in his nostrils. Laika Cardinal. Instantly, he got the feeling that this would be the start of new and big things for him. Obviously, how could he the man, be expected to give up his own name, without getting anything in return? He definitely would have to find a subtle way to request that this name change be in his best interest and for sure by the time he had arrived at the house, he already had a good reason.

Mr Cardinal met him at the door of his study, just the two of them this time.

"So, Laika have you made a decision?"

Laika said in a very subdued voice, "As much as I love your daughter, sir," he had to practise several times before he stopped gagging on the word 'love'. "This is a very hard choice, which I am sure a man like yourself can understand! You see, I am my parents' only child and I promised both my father and grandfather that I would always honour their name. Undeniably, I was expected to bear the family name for posterity."

Mr Cardinal, looked very perturbed (Laika thought that he had been too convincing and this man would change his mind) but in a moment seemed to have decided.

He said, "I completely understand, Laika, so here's what I am suggesting to make amends; my wife and I agreed that since you are the first son-in-law and indeed our first son—"

"Thank you, sir, that's a huge honour!"

With an impatient wave of the hand, he continued, as if what he had to say was so very important that he couldn't afford to be interrupted.

"You and Mary Ann, as long as the two of you remain married, will inherit all our earthly possessions and, based on your proven track record, I know that we are leaving everything – this house, the farm, our business dealings – in capable hands."

Laika was so genuinely moved, so overcome with emotions that he had not felt in a long time – quite possibly never – that he couldn't speak for about ten minutes. He couldn't trust himself to speak. He had not cried in many years (not since Lawrence) and he could not afford to right now. No one had ever entrusted him with anything of value. No one had ever offered to leave him an inheritance, not even his own father. Despite Laika's plotting, the man's tone, his words and demeanour offered a kindness, a warmth and a tenderness that Laika had not experienced in years. Certainly, not since his grandmother Mary was alive. He was very unprepared for the generosity and altruism being extended to him. It took, the usually inured Laika a few minutes to pull himself together. He was absolutely speechless and would be beholden to this man, his new father in law forever. He was so unprepared for how things turned out, it had the effect on him of being swept off his feet, like being in an earthquake and at the end, discovering that everything had shifted from their original position. Because, indeed, this was a huge shift in the trajectory of his life. He pictured his life going one way and in less than an hour, it had gone in a completely different way. Grandma Mary was right, *miracles happen each and every day, even when you don't have enough sense to believe.*

Everything in him changed that day and for years he was in shock about the unwavering goodness of these people. These people who gave so much and asked for so very little. These people who were always happy to see him, even years after he had been married to Mary Ann, they were always happy to speak with him and showed interest in everything that he had to say. The Cardinals always showed that they valued him and his opinion. For the first time in his life, Laika felt like he was home, finally home and made a personal pledge in that moment, to be a better person, to honour Mary Ann, to honour this man and to honour this moment.

Laika Cardinal thrived more than he ever thought possible which goes to show how just the idea that he was loved and accepted made him grow. People most often will become the best version of themselves if they know that they are loved. That's basically al Laika needed all his life; to know that he is loved and accepted.

Laika achieved his dream, got the girl; eventually, moved into the big beautiful house which was still not Emersyn. He did his best to make her over into Emersyn but it was still not the same. Mary Ann decided to call the house Beryl, to honour her mum's passing and highlight Laika's heritage. Mary Ann proved to be a loving and devoted wife and mother. She loved some of the pain away, only some, because some hurts are too deeply rooted to be so easily medicated. In tender moments, he even shared with Mary Ann stories about his grandmother who loved him more than anyone else did in his childhood. But not the unlovely parts of his story, just the parts that had carried him through hard times in his life. Laika did keep his word and never did anything untoward ever again. He was inspired to be an honourable man. Eventually, the Cardinals stopped looking for Avant and via Laika assumed that she had eloped. That was quite unrealistic but Laika; despite his changed persona, was still a Whiley in deed and in truth.

Laika begot Kam (a combination of Laika + Mary Ann) and Macy. Kam begot Gabriel, Sal and Colton. Colton begot Tandey, Tandey begot Tandey Jr or TJ and Sakine. TJ begot Athena and Oswald. Oswald begot Ava, Avery and Amoury. These are the generations of Laika and Mary Ann Cardinal a lineage that have survived the test of time.

Chapter Ten
No Stealing from the Past

"Where does seeking justice end and seeking vengeance begin?" Paula Stokes

Amoury Cardinal

Amoury is the great, great, great, great, great, great, great grandson of Laika Cardinal. Laika was the son of Lance, Acram's son, but was given the surname of his maternal grandmother. The same Laika who felt that he had been unfairly treated, sought to exact revenge but had to flee Shrove. In spite of all his good fortune; Laika had never forgotten that.

All in all, Laika lived a very good life, lived to a ripe old age, in the north (where he had fled) and being a son of Lance's did have the ingenuity and had developed the work ethic to achieve success. Therefore, being prudent, he was able to leave a sizeable inheritance for his children and children's children. Thankfully, now that he had come to understand unconditional love through the efforts of the Cardinals, he did try to make amends. However, he left an inheritance along with strict instructions that they had to destroy the Whileys and take possession of Emersyn at all costs.

Eventually, in his twilight years – a second childhood – when facades fail and posturing exhausting, he did tell them the tale of how he had to flee – minus the detail of having killed Lawrence, he was merely getting older, he was in no way decrepit – because he was being persecuted by his brethren. From a child, he often visualised himself as a modern-day Joseph. He presented his story, time after time; an innocent man, who was born in the wrong time period and had been barred from his father's legacy by unfair siblings and a skin colour that he had no control over. This narrative like a mantle, a cloak of many colours, had been passed on from generation to generation. Each generation trying it on, seeing how well it fit; some could not bear its weight; while still others found it oppressive and confining.

In the fullness of time, it was soon Amoury's turn to try on this cloak. Amoury, a university graduate, with a Bachelor's degree in Natural Sciences and a Masters in Anthropology has been on a quest to execute the mission of his father and grandfathers before him. By nature, a rationalist and who was compelled by reasons of his own to accomplish this goal. He is fundamentally very curious by nature; therefore, he also wanted to meet his *other* family. Through his studies, he had learned about the ravages and the indignities of slavery and his youthful passion convinced him that righting a wrong in his own family was not only a familial inclination but a moral obligation to humanity as well. An idealist as well, who harboured a fantasy of going down in history as the one to amalgamate his family. Not to mention the fact that, he had never learned much from his father or grandfather about the Whiley side of his origin story so he grasped this opportunity believing that this was a genius way to learn about his origin story, prior to Laika Cardinal working with Burnam.

Amoury, through his studies had visited South Africa but he saw that as a call to unearth his past. However, he did not know where to start but he felt a strong connection to the land and the people. He also acquired a great love for mountains as while there he had visited several of the many mammoth mountains in South Africa. He felt at peace while trekking, through the mountains, a oneness with nature, a deep settled peace that he feels nowhere else. Looking on the few images online of Emersyn, he was thrilled to see that a mountain actually *held* Emersyn in place; as he liked to think of the magnificent collection of hills surrounding Emersyn. Ensuring that she moved deeply rooted to the land and never facing upheavals from any acts of nature.

So far, he has been the only one who had a pragmatic plan that got him this close to the Whileys. He had tried for years to reach out to them, but kept running into a wall. They seem to have a huge firewall around them that made access to them almost impenetrable. Finally, he read in the paper that young Mason Whiley was about to take over the family business and later that his dad Cahal Whiley had transitioned. Amoury felt like this was an opportune moment, the most fitting and appropriate time to strike when he would have the full attention of the young Whiley and not the older Whiley with all his prejudices, biases and potentially his bigotry. He hoped that the younger Whiley would be more receptive and responsive to the changing times. Most of the older generations in the south had grown up knowing only one way of existing so he really did not blame them for their enclosed minds but he did think it was the responsibility of the young to change and adapt to these ever-changing times.

On his quest, he soon realised that Mason was just a few years older than him and with the same startlingly green eyes. People were always amazed that he had such relatively dark skin but such brilliant green eyes. He often joked that, his green eyes were his family gems. These gems have often separated him from his peers and included him among people he never thought would have accepted him. He considered himself a walking epistle of the harmony that can and should exist among the races.

A few months ago, through a stroke of good luck, he got in touch with an individual close to Mason, who was just as hell bent on revenge and together they crafted a plan that got him in touch with Mason Whiley, the heir apparent who was currently in charge of Emersyn. There was also an 'insider' who opted to remain anonymous, but was the key in giving him access to Mason. In a way, he felt for Mason, having an enemy so close and being unaware of it. Amoury had to remind himself that; essentially, that was not his problem, that was not his concern. After many phone calls, he had finally gotten a date and a time to meet Mason at Emersyn. He could not believe that having heard so much about Emersyn all his life and seeing a few pictures online (the Whileys have always been a very private people) he couldn't blame them for that. Equally important, is the fact that he was going to visit Shrove, the place Laika was born and grew up. In his mind, Shrove had become his ancestral land. A place where he hoped to connect with his roots and possibly meet other people who look like him.

At last the day came when he was supposed to fly into Shrove and meet his family who had absolutely no idea that he was related to them and how could they? He's not white; hence, not considered a part of their bloodline. The night before, like a kid's first trip to Disney World, Amoury couldn't contain his excitement. He even had a dream that he was standing on the ground floor landing at Emersyn but the entire area was covered by bones, old bones. On waking up, he could remember every detail of the dream but he ascribed it to nervous tension messing with his mind.

Mason had made plans with Amoury to meet him at the airport and have a quick lunch. They would leave the heavy stuff for the following morning when a driver would bring Amoury to Emersyn. Immediately, after lunch, Mason would have his driver take him to a hotel in town and Amoury was quite fine with that plan of action. Shrove is sure far away from the maddening crowd that

79

Amoury is accustomed to. He caught the red eye and never got there until noon. He was exhausted.

When Amoury entered the waiting area, he had to pause for a while – Mason's undeniable resemblance to the pictures of his ancestor Laika and those enigmatic green eyes, hanging in the foyer at his house, Beryl – took his breath away. He had to take a few minutes to centre himself before approaching, it was actually like seeing one of his siblings, or a cousin since a few of them through the generations had inherited Laika's green gems – minus his complexion of course.

Unquestionably, Mason was hard to miss not only because of his height, blonde hair and green eyes, stylish cowboy hat and fancy knee-high leather boots but also his aura even from this far away was reminiscent of old-world charm and affluence. He was the very embodiment of old money and animal magnetism as was quite obvious, even from his gait and stance that he is an alpha male. One who would stark his prey and devour it efficiently. That being said, there was also a gentility to him that could only come from breeding. Yes, Mason was definitely from the right stock.

It was not quite summer time yet, still spring but based on a cursory glance, quite a few people had embraced this mode of dressing (knee high leather boots). But by far, Mason was the most striking. Fundamentally, Amoury decided that it was his confidence that set him apart from other men and made him the most distinguished. A confidence that came from knowing his lineage which was linked to his destiny.

****

I approached Mason from behind, a tactic designed to give me the upper hand in this situation.

"Hi, Mason."

At his name Mason turns around quickly, but unintentionally pauses, visibly shaken at the sight of me. He kept gazing into my green eyes; green eyes embracing green eyes. I bet he was astounded to see green eyes matched with dark skin. I had not inherited Laika's blonde curls but my hair is light brown with big curls. This floors people every time and it never fails to amuse me.

Eventually, southern hospitality prevails and he composes himself. Clearly, he was a man accustomed to being in control of even the most exacting circumstances that he had learned a long time ago how to school his emotions.

He gripped my hand tightly (left hand gripping left hand) and said in his southern drawl, "Hey there, nice to meet you finally, Amoury. My car is waiting."

The irony here is, I was supposed to have the upper hand, but knew right away that this is a man accustomed to having the advantage; being in the dominant position – an alpha male. I could not help but be amazed at his natural take charge attitude, it seemed like all his life he had been groomed for his place in the world. I also can't help but wonder what I have gotten myself into, in his presence, I feel like a tiny mountain goat lost in the Appalachian Mountains.

On our way to his car, a Jaguar, we indulge in small talk. Something I hate immensely and I could tell he abhors this as well, as he is palpably straining against the pressure of the exchange and being pulled out of character. Obviously, he was a man who habitually takes the lead in situations like these and life in general. In fact, my student hand isstill reeling from his alpha male grip. We get to the restaurant – even from a distance, one could tell that this is where all the rich people congregate, a few of them greeting him warmly, a sign of comradery; an old boys club as well.

We had a great lunch and I offered to pay but he said loudly, "I wouldn't hear of it. Your money is no good here, so put it away."

We both laugh again! I have to get accustomed to his powerful voice on the double, I cannot keep jumping every time he speaks. Invariably, that would be bad for business. Decidedly, I could really get use to his droning which I feel is a bit deceptive as it gives an impression of being overly causal and laidback, which this man plainly isn't. By the time we had finished our entree, I know that he had summed me up well. I was beginning to wonder what I had gotten myself into. Certainly, the Mason on the phone, cordial and expressive is a completely different one from this gentleman here because this Mason has decided to go into business with me. He is not about to invest in someone or anything that is not as solid as the walls he has around him. I get the distinct impression that he is not to be played with and he will be a formidable opponent.

Before the cheque came, somehow, I had been gently cajoled into visiting Emersyn and the farm, straight away. I thought that I would just go to my hotel, take a long shower after my exhausting flight and get some rest so that I would be mentally and emotionally ready to meet Emersyn – the place I heard so much about while growing up because Laika made sure that successive generations passed on the wonder that was Emersyn to the next. Despite being severely fatigued, I would not want to give Mason the impression that I am unstable by opposing his proposal; unequivocally, that would not be good for business and I perceived that this was a good sign.

All the way there, I tried to prepare myself. Also, I reflected on one of the stories that my dad told me that his dad had passed on to him. Laika said that his grandfather Acram, had won Emersyn in a card game but he was always quick to add, 'Don't let that tacky detail fool you!' As we approach, even from a distance and despite the great iron gates, I see her looming in the distance, like a great gem, an emerald being worn by an Ethiopian princess. I had to catch my breath. At this Mason looks at me, offers a smile and declares, 'A thing of great beauty isn't she!' I could only nod my approval.

Emersyn is anything but Tacky. She stands majestic with the mountain range as a frame for her existence. There were giant magnolias about 40 feet tall at the time, which had been planted in their infancy, coupled with many varieties of flowers; among them, many different varieties of roses. When the roses were in bloom, their scent mingled with the apple blossoms and wafted for miles around. It was always as if Emersyn was being cuddled by all those many and various fragrances. You can always tell when you are close to Emersyn by the pleasant aroma of either apples, apple blossoms, roses or a combination. The apple orchards are also something to admire. They stand sublime like footmen gazing up at their leader. Just being in the environment inspires such bliss, that everyone simply accepted that once you set foot in Emersyn there was no going back to being the same.

And that was just the outside description. I was so anxious to see inside.

Chapter Eleven
Appearance vs Reality

"Appearance is something absolute, but reality is not that way…" – *Dalai Lama*

Mason

I really had no intention of inviting Amoury to Emersyn today and generally I am never impulsive about my decisions. I have never met anyone as hypnotic as this gentleman. But there is just something about this black man with green eyes. Sure, I have seen this phenomenon right here in Shrove, there are some people like him, but it is not just that, it is his natural charm and intellect. He bears an aura of old school wisdom that I always find very irresistible, in some ways he reminds me of Val. I have been watching him all afternoon and everything about him screams safe so by the time we had returned to the car, I had made up my mind. I don't know if it is his mesmerising green eyes so much like mine and my siblings or just his dignified mannerism. This Amoury fellow seems so genuine and despite his apparent diffidence carries an aura of old school charm, of nobility even. Let's hope Mama sees Amoury in this same vein because I still have not informed her of my decision to go into business with him.

We get to Emersyn a few hours before supper and not a moment too soon. The sky had turned black on the way here and now I hear a clap of thunder, followed by a peel of lighting signalling the deluge to come. In these parts, it can rain an ocean in a few hours. I leave Amoury on the ground floor landing to inform every one that we will be having a guest dinner. Also, we have many unused rooms so for the week that he will be visiting, I fully intend to invite him to stay here at Emersyn instead of staying in an unknown hotel room, which is probably unhygienic as well. Plus, with this rain coming, it might be best for him to just stay here; indeed, for the night and for the week, while we sort through our business interests.

I tell Avery first and he is fine with it. It actually seems like he was in the middle of a heated phone conversation that I had interrupted so he was anxious for me to leave. I inform everyone; including Mauve, who is thrilled that I have invited Amoury home.

She said, "Finally, someone different and interesting to converse with at supper instead of the same bland conversations."

Val seems undecided.

She said, "Wow! That was quick. From being dubious one week, to inviting him home for dinner the next. I hope you are not moving too quickly, make sure you remember to be prudent."

I assure her that it will be OK and she'll understand my decision once she meets him.

She said, "Why so secretive, bro?"

And I tell her it's best if she sees him for herself.

The last person on my list is Mama. I say a quick prayer and ensure that Chloe isn't milling around. I check Chloe's usual spots, as she is always hiding in a corner near mama's door, waiting to pounce on an opportunity to get in. For some ungodly reason Chloe thrives on aggravating my mother. I absolutely do not want her provoking Mama to wrath at a time like this. I need Mama to be in a good mood, to be focused and attentive for what I am about to tell her. The success or failure of my whole business deal potentially rests on Mama's comportment. I look everywhere and there is no sign of Chloe, so I knock quietly on her door and enter quickly before I change my mind.

****

Amoury

The rain that has been threatening now comes down in buckets, with thunder and lightning as its musical accompaniment. Where I come from, it never rains this much. It is almost scary. I don't think the family was expecting me. I am grateful for this moment of solitude – as Mason said, there are seven of them, plus wives and children and his mum Beatrice – so that I can clarify my thoughts in private, at least for now. My home, Beryl, is spectacular but really, she pales in comparison to Emersyn. Emersyn's exterior is grand but inside is breathtakingly magnificent. When I walked in, I had to catch my breath again and make an effort to control my breathing. Thankfully, Mason was so focused on locating his family that he didn't notice my visceral reaction. But I am sure, he is accustomed to people being astounded by the unparalleled jewel, which is

Emersyn. Somehow, I had an inexplicable sensation that I was coming home, just like I felt when I stepped off the plane in Johannesburg, South Africa, I felt like I was home. I imagined that I had journeyed all my life to find my way home.

Mason leaves me on the ground floor landing to go inform his family of my arrival. This is exactly like my dream last night; minus the bones. Thankfully, there are no bones, just the picturesque representation of splendour, magnificence and grandeur. Simply, walking through the front doors remind me of a trip I had taken to South Africa as an undergrad while working on my anthropology thesis. My cohorts and I visited Cape Town, South Africa. We had the extreme pleasure of visiting Stratford Castle; the architecture, the artwork, the décor was mind blowing; added to that, the ambiance, the palpable feel like you are actually in the presence of royalty. The antiquity of the place added to its tantalising charm like a rare gem wore by an Ethiopian princess. I felt like I was walking into a modern-day fairy-tale. Like the heady sense of déjà vu, this was the atmosphere that emanated out to me as I walked into the foyer of Emersyn, it was more like floating than walking. The character of Emersyn is so much like a castle, on a hill in the countryside surrounded by the right, rich variety of flora and fauna, it almost seems out of place in this setting. However, like a rare plant, in a distant land, Emersyn has decided to merge with her surroundings and create a synthesis where she emerges as the dominant amalgam. Emersyn is like one of those formidable individuals who no matter where you place them, they flourish. Hence, they will never be outshined, excelled, surpassed by any other, they will unfailingly leave an indelible impression on all who come into contact with them and invariably they will be unforgettable.

The wide rolling staircases are both overwhelming and intimidating. The furnishing both modern and sophisticated. The drapes a rich gold colour, I'm not sure what colour to ascribe other than that (I have never been good at identifying colours) it is full, flowing elegance. While I was looking at the drapery and marvelling that in itself and certainly by itself, it is a work of art, a small cat came tumbling out from among the network of fabric. He or she stretched, looked at me without blinking for what seemed like an eternity, then started cleaning itself. Once that chore was complete, she came close enough so I could observe her more carefully. She sniffed me a few times, meowed a couple of times and then started rubbing against my leg. The very little I know about cats, is that this action indicates that she has accepted me in her house and she is therefore, memorising my scent combining it with hers. I took that as a good omen, that the rest of the family, my family will accept me as well with open arms. My entire plan rests solely on getting the Whileys to trust me.

Shortly after the cat leaves, while I was looking at the many elaborate art pieces that line the wall – the one closest to me a Van Gogh, purple long stemmed flowers – an exquisite young lady descends the stairs. Her green eyes accentuated by the orange scarf tied around her neck, which gave the impression of waves around her neck, the scarf matched the now familiar knee-high boots. I could literally drown in those tantalising green eyes. She paused at the foot of the stairs, assessing me, before she came over, extending a slender, toned and tanned hand to me.

She said, "Hi, my name is Valencia, but everyone calls me Val. You must be Amoury. Welcome to Emersyn. I am Mason's youngest sister."

My throat went dry, whatever moisture should have been in my throat now appeared on my palms. I barely managed to say, 'Thank you! The pleasure is all mine,' before my voice broke, like when I was a teenager. This was so embarrassing.

I was relieved when she said, "That piece is a Van Gogh, it's called Irises. It is said that he actually created it while he was in an asylum. Apparently, he was going through a dark time in his life when he was self-mutilating, so he chose to voluntarily check himself into an asylum. But despite the turmoil in his mind, it had the presence of mind to still capture nature at its best."

I murmured, not trusting my voice, "That's intriguing."

She said, "Has Mason shown you around?"

I shake my head in the negative.

She said, "Come with me, I'll give you the grand tour. I'll entertain you until Mason gets back from his errands."

Right away I knew that I would go anywhere with her. Thankfully, this generally means that, the person doing the showing would be doing most of the talking and all I had to do was just look impressed, smile, nod my head and say 'yes, really'. This would definitely not be hard. I managed to shake my head in the affirmative. Fortunately, she asked if I would like something to drink. Again, shaking my head, not yet ready to trust myself to speak, she must think I am a dullard of the highest order.

In just a brief moment, meeting these Whileys have robbed me of my essence. I am amazed at how their mere presence renders me either mute or absent from myself. The imposter syndrome is slowly kicking in. I am not even going to lie, I thought I was mentally prepared for this quest but it is so easy to be swept away amidst all this opulence and grandiosity. No wonder Laika felt out of his depths.

She offers me a glorious pink liquid. She described it as, a type of sparkling non-alcoholic wine made right here at Emersyn, from the over ripe apples. I know I am going to thoroughly enjoy this visit because if this is how their non-alcoholic wine taste, I can scarcely wait to taste their alcoholic variety. However, of necessity I will have to repeatedly remind myself of my mission here. I can already tell that this is going to be very hard. I was fully expecting old, decrepit people, then I met Mason, the cat, now Val. I can tell my victory is going to be hard fought, if I can keep focused on my mission because just like Emersyn, Val is indeed exquisite.

****

Mason

I thought actually having Amoury here in the house would invariably plead my cause for me, give me some traction; but needless to say, I was hoping against hope. Mama, would not budge. Thank heavens these old walls are as thick as thieves.

She kept screaming at me, "How dare you bring that nigger into this house! How dare you try to deface this house by inviting him here! Your father must be turning in his grave! Never in my lifetime has a nigger set foot in this house."

I tried to reason with her but she would not listen. She was by far too enraged! Eventually, I had to join her in the screaming fest because I could not standby another minute and listen to her calling such a decent fellow the N word. I don't care how old school or how upset Mama is, that is just so uncalled for and unnecessarily cruel. I guess there is no changing years of a romanticised notion of supremacy.

After that, she resorted to blackmail.

"By going into business with this person, and bringing him here, you are signing my death warrant. For sure this is going to be the death of me!"

Mama is always predicting her death. I have watched her do it countless times both with Dad and my other siblings, it has become a running joke in the family. 'You are going to be the death of Mum,' or 'You will inspire Mum's demise with that idea.' Quite morbid, but a joke nonetheless.

That being said, I can never remember seeing mama so furious. I had to shout at her over and over again to calm down. She had turned blood red and the prominent vein in her neck was palpitating. In the end, she threw me out of her room with a disclaimer.

"I'd rather sleep with that disgusting Chloe in my bed for the rest of my life, than sleep in this house with that person."

At least she had ceased and desist from the obnoxious name calling. You would think that he has actually stolen something from her. In the end, she refused to join us for dinner. She locked herself in her room to emphasise her displeasure and to protest my decision. There was nothing left to do but inform the staff that they should serve Mama her dinner in her room and prepare an extra place setting.

This was going to prove to be a much more difficult week than I have anticipated.

Everyone is on board with having a guest for the week. They all were aware that I had informed them as a courtesy and not because I was seeking permission, I made that quite clear. I was happy to see that Val had met Amoury and had shown him around. I introduced him to everyone and they all seemed enthusiastic to meet him; except Gabe. But Gabe is somewhat of a pessimist so I am not really surprised. Amethyst seemed the most interested. I guess that's a great sign.

Shortly before dinner once everyone had gathered and we are about to start the appetiser, my youngest who generally eats with the other kids in the adjacent hall, came flying into the room, almost tipping over a chair, luckily falling in my lap.

I said, "Slow down, Marla. I've told you many times that you are going to hurt yourself!"

She caught her breath and said, "Dad... Daddy... guess what happened?"

I waited for her to proceed.

She said, "Chloe fell into the toilet and we're afraid to get her out! She keeps crying and splashing around."

Someone said, "That goddam Chloe again!"

Someone else said, "Maybe we should just flush her!"

As I left the room with Marla, a heated discussion had started about animal cruelty and the cruelty of animals to their humans. Amoury must think that we are a set of morons.

I excused myself to investigate, signalling to Mauve that she needs to stay and hold down the fort. When I finally get there, I extricated a now wailing and shivering Chloe from the toilet and had her wrapped in a towel, I sought to ascertain what had happened. By now all the kids were excitedly gathered around me each trying to explain what happened at the same time. Some sympathetic towards Chloe while others blamed her for her tom foolery. I was really starting to get a headache. I had to wait for several minutes for them to calm down and even then they insisted on telling the tale together. From what I could gather, the staff had followed my instructions and brought Mama's meal to her and at her insistence had left the tray by her door. Mama can be so spiteful at times. Now here comes Chloe, sniffing around and discovering that it was her favourite – rice – she had a feast. Then, naturally she started barfing and one of the kids decided to hold her over the toilet so she wouldn't make a mess, she kept squirming and voila, she fell into the toilet.

What am I going to do with Mama and Chloe?

I managed to get Chloe dry using a hair dryer as suggested by one of the older kids and dispatched them to their eating area. My headache had gotten worse. I really needed a minute to compose myself, but there was no time. Dinner was already late because of me. When I returned to the dining room, they were all waiting on me, some even had jokes.

"Did you flush her?"

This is going to be a long night. At least Amoury seemed to be having a good time, when I entered the room, my eyes found him and he was engrossed in a conversation with Amelia. The worse possible person for him to be talking with but at least Emery is nearby so he could hopefully put a stop to her madness before it begins.

Chapter Twelve
A Unique Gift

"Life is a lively process of becoming." – Douglas MacArthur

Valencia

Of all the Whiley children, Val has always manifested Aunt Faith the most. She is always kind and compassionate, always eager to help; she definitely has Faith's temperament. Notably, despite the fact that she is the youngest girl in the family, a position and a title traditionally regarded with contempt – after Mason and sometimes even before Mason – generally; she is the one her siblings would seek advice from. Things were not always like this for her, there once was a time when she felt like an outcast in her own family and the subject of immense scepticism. She didn't always feel protected or welcomed by her family. However, things are different now. Even Mason, always seems so grateful for the fact of his sister's counsel, one less thing for him to worry about. He sometimes wonders aloud what would happen should Val decide to marry. It's been a long journey to inclusion but it was all worth it.

When Val was seven years old, she had a near death experience which seemed to have triggered in her a connection to the supernatural. On a very sunny and hot afternoon, when all the plants seemed to have wilted under the blaze of the mid-afternoon sun, when all the little animals had scurried away to their underground sanctuary, young Val, persuaded her mum to take her to her friend Quin's house, so she could have a play date. Beatrice did not really want to take her, not wanting to leave the comfort of her living room to face the angry glare of the sun. However, Val was able to convince her mum through her whining and complaining. There had always been an open invitation to Quin's house from as far back as kindergarten.

On this particular day, despite the fact that she had had many swimming lessons; in fact, a competent swimmer and was wearing appropriate gear, she felt like she was being held obviously against her will, under the water. Obviously, she was pushing back against the force holding her against her will and fortunately, just when she thought that was going under for the last time and indeed would, die in her youth; Quin's mum noticed right in time and came to her rescue. This was a very traumatic situation for her. After that encounter, she would at times see things that others could not and heard things that she sometimes found difficult to explain. Also, she would sometimes know things before they happen which would be so problematic because most rational individuals like to know the whys and the wherefores; however, most times she couldn't supply that information. This new and sudden ability was the beginning of a life of isolation as second grade girls were never thrilled to hear that their dearly departed grandparent, aunt or uncle were still visiting their rooms occasionally. This continued through elementary school and by high school she was known as the *ghost finder*. Certainly, a ghost would be sure to appear when Val was around. At first, she was really, really unhappy about this new turn of events but overtime came to embrace it as a gift because sometimes she would be compelled to inform people of the presence of a loved one who they were worried about and this would soon lead to peace for both the quick and the dead. Naturally, many people would not publicly admit to this but secretly they would view her as a gem and thanked her profusely for her help. Some took more persuasion than others which invariably would leave Val exhausted because by nature, she was an introvert so this new time pastime really took her out of her comfort zone.

Val's parents did not know what to make of her newly discovered talent, or skill – they didn't even know what to call it. At first, they ignored her pronouncements that odd people were standing *there* when no one else could see them. This certainly made for some really unsettling conversations and disturbing moments. They could not take her anywhere, not on any vacations because invariably an apparition would appear which would lead to great disquiet among her siblings. Not to mention friends, they never had many friends to begin with but the few they did have found little Val too disconcerting. Because one thing is for sure, humans never really want to face their mortality and that is exactly what Val was unwittingly asking them to acknowledge.

Finally, her parents were forced to give up a lot of their avocations; among those, their penchant for extravagance. Cahal and Beatrice Whiley were well-known in Shrove to throw lavish parties. In fact, they were the only Whileys to take any interest in these soirees, no one before their generation or after ever took any pleasure in this mode of recreation. After a while, they had to put an end to these amusements as they came to realise that a lot of people only came to gawk at Val like a zoo animal. They would ask, 'Is she here?' And by she everyone knew they were referring to Val. Little Val's vocation had preceded her; therefore, in a bid to protect their child, her parents decided that a quiet, less public life was best. Cahal was fine with it, he didn't much like a lot of the people who came but this was devastating for Beatrice. She secretly missed her ball dresses and her grand entrances. Beatrice so thoroughly enjoyed seeing the desire in other people's eyes; indeed, women envied her and men wanted her. She felt like a life of being the centre of attention was the life she was meant to have.

Subsequently, she started to resent Val and Val being the sensitive child that she was could sense her mother's discontentment and disapproval. Val would argue that, it is not like I want this for myself; not even a case where I went looking for it myself. This naturally drove a wedge between them at a time when Val needed her mum the most. Val tried her best to be 'normal' but she just could not control this new phenomenon that had so unexpectedly entered her life. Overtime, she came to resent her mum and really had to try hard to be in her presence. Val even wanted to move away after college; but where would she go? The world is so big; this would be inviting a whole lot more encounters of the weird kind in her life. She decided to stick with the evil that she knew. She reasoned that Emersyn was so big that she really did have to have much contact with her mum. She would forego the mandatory dinners. It was a very long time before she started having supper with her family again.

This happened after she started having troubling headaches; these headaches were often debilitating. She did every test in the book and all of them came back negative. All her doctors were flabbergasted. No one knew exactly what had triggered these headaches or how to treat them. She would often just sit in a darkened room for days before these headaches went away. Eventually, her only friend for as far back as she could remember, advised her to see a psychologist, which her doctors had hinted at but knowing the senior Whileys peculiarities, they did not want to over-emphasise such a thing. This notion set off fireworks in her very traditional family.

Her father declared loudly enough for everyone to hear to deter anyone with similar notions, "Not one Whiley, absolutely none, in the history of Whileys has ever paid a shrink a dime! Never!"

He went on to emphasise, "I am not about to give my hard-earned money to any shrink."

"Absolutely not!"

Her mum was mortified.

"What would people think? How would she face anyone in town? Because surely, everyone will know!"

On top of everything else that had gone horribly wrong in her life, she could not face 'being mocked by people who are beneath me'. Her siblings were far more supportive, they argued that, that was an archaic idea that people shouldn't seek help when needed; regardless of the source. Needless to say, there was a lot of yelling, which did not help her headaches. Finally, her parents relented, after much pressure from their children; also, the frequency of the headaches had intensified because of all the yelling and screaming in the house. Reluctantly, they agreed for her to see a shrink, one who came highly recommended, just not anyone in town. Val had to move out of state to get the help that she so desperately needed.

As fate would have it, moving out of state was the best thing she ever did. That's when she met Dr Evelyn Mercado or Evie as she preferred to be called, who completely changed her world view. Dr Mercado was not only a counsellor but also a Christian who came highly recommended but she was also black. Growing up in Shrove and the family that she grew up would normally apply some amount of stress for Val but she was too weary to care. Plus, Dr Evie was the top female in her profession and had been practicing over ten years.

Mercado is an empath and that helped her to connect with her patients. She comes to this profession as a mother who lost her only child in a car accident; along with her husband of ten years. Grief has really taught her compassion which really resonates with her patients. Sometimes her strategy is often unorthodox; however, most of her patients do well and remain friends even after treatment. She struggled so much with her own grief; so much so, that she started to experience chronic sciatica nerve pain. Of such, she exhausted all her medical options that included physiotherapy, massage therapy and working with a chiropractor. When none of that helped, she started to explore emotional therapy and that's when she came across a theory called mind-body pain. That seemingly, simple diagnosis changed her life. She then had to reckon with the fact her emotional trauma had so deeply inflicted her physical body. There was so much work to be done and some days it was exceptionally hard but she learned to push through the pain.

Evelyn perceives every encounter with a new patient as a *Cornelius Meeting,* and lives by the mantra, *all things work together for good;* therefore, everything had been orchestrated from *the foundation of the world.* Evie postulates that nothing, no situation was either good or bad, but it all came down to perspective and how we interacted with the situation. Granted, coming from a small town, although being a college graduate, some of the ideas were very confusing for Val; hence, difficult to grasp. Val had to confront her own prejudices in order to be able to benefit from the sessions.

The other monumental paradigm shift that came into her life was that, Dr Evelyn taught her to embrace her 'gift' and for the very first time in her life, someone actually referred to her 'condition' as a gift; not a curse, not a burden, not something that she should be embarrassed about but a gift from God. Initially, that was a very difficult concept for Val to embrace because by then she was exhausted after years of fighting against herself, combating her most natural inclinations.

Plus, she vehemently argued, why would a supposedly benevolent God place such a burden on such a young child? Why would he destroy her life, removing all her friends at such a tender age? Those sessions were really hard and left her drained. Evie rebutted with the notion that her gift led to their meeting which was ordained to have happened, for her grooming she needed to be isolated and to be elevated she had to be rejected. Her doctor was of the view, that her purpose was far greater than the boundaries of Shrove and in order to excel to her highest self, she had to remove the boundaries that living Shrove, her parents and even through her own actions that she had placed on herself. Apparently, she also needed to love herself, forgive herself and speak lovingly to herself as this was a fundamentally part of her healing. More importantly, she had to let dead things go and awaken other important things in her life which were about to die.

Sometimes, Val found herself wondering, what was the point as she often left her sessions even more perturbed and with a bigger headache than what she started the day with. These ideas were too novel and too inflated for her limited understanding. The other thing that Val hated was the fact that these sessions were often repetitive.

Evie informed her, "These sessions are repetitive because you need to open new neural pathways in your brain for change to happen. We cannot change

DNA or any natural predisposition but we can rewire the brain into being more receptive and responsive to new ideas."

Clearly being a Whiley had predisposed her to a whole lot of misnomers and had locked specific pathways in her brain that would generally respond to change.

In the fullness of time, after much love and support from Evie, she slowly decided to accept her portion in life. Even more slowly she came to understand that her affliction was not physical. She became aware of the fact that, she had so much resentment for her mum over the years that her resentment started to impact her emotionally and her headaches were a physical reaction to the emotional pain of losing a connection to her mum so early in life. Therefore, in order for healing to happen, she had to consciously resolve to forgive her mum, for not being able to love her through the most difficult, life changing event that she had to deal with. She had to learn to cope on her own because her mum chose to abandon her during this most critical time. Certainly, for not loving her enough to see her through the darkest times in her life.

Indeed Val was a changed person and was the first and only Whiley to ever enter into counselling, a notion which her father never failed to remind her of. For the first time since she was seven, she was happy again. She started enjoying her life more, looked forward to the future and gradually all the headaches went. As life is sometimes, after years of incapacitating pain, she woke up one day and all the pain was gone. For the first time ever, she saw her Aunt Faith, very clearly; previously, she had only heard her voice.

Aunt Faith said, "I knew you could do it. I've been cheering for this whole time. Now go back to Emersyn and make the change happen."

This left her even more confused than her counselling had. But in an instant Aunt Faith was gone leaving her to figure out the change that was necessary. After discussing the sudden appearance of her deceased aunt with Evie, she decided to let that episode go as Evie convinced her that when the time came for said change, she would know and most importantly she would be ready.

Val couldn't wait to get home to have a heart to heart with her mum. In the beginning, she was worried about upsetting her mum and that she might not actually get an apology or worse that her mother wouldn't actually allow her to finish. However, both her and Evie prayed about it and got confirmation that all would be well. That was the other thing that she had learned from her therapist, how to pray. She came from a deeply religious family which meant church every

Sunday, every holiday, special occasions, funerals, weddings; prayer at meal time. But essentially, in terms of embracing the practicality of prayer, the application of the Word of God, this is a whole new experience for her and one that she thoroughly embraced. Evie calls this practice honouring her faith and Val believes that this something which has been absent from her life but was indeed necessary for her overall well-being. She has used the scriptures to ground herself and settle her fears. Also, she has learned how to pray and wait; instead of rushing into situations, acting on impulse and then regretting her decision.

The discussion with her mum was not an easy one. But she had approached the situation prayerful and was confident that this was the right path to take, the right thing to do. Initially, her mum was hesitant about meeting with her and in fairness to her, she didn't know what to expect. That was the other lesson Val learned to be fair to not only herself but to her parents as well; specifically, her mum. She now understood that her mum was functioning on the information that she had which she had learned from her *own* parents. She came to see her mum as a person with her own idiosyncrasies and insecurities. She accepted that like anyone else, her mum had fears and those fears prevented her from being the best that she could be. So, they arranged to meet at the poplar tree. A very unusual place to meet but Val felt like it would give the privacy needed to say what needed to be said and set the ambiance for complete transparency.

She started out by saying, "Hi, Mum, thanks for meeting me here."

Beatrice said, "You did not leave me much choice, did you?"

"Mum, I am not forcing you to be here. I apologise if that is how my request caused you to feel. You can leave anytime that you like but I am really hoping that you will stay so that we can both put a close to this chapter of our lives."

"OK! If this is important to you, I'll stay for your sake."

"Thanks, Mum. At first, I thought of writing you a letter but then I thought that words mean different things to different people. Therefore, I decided to speak with you face to face so that if at any time, I say anything that you disagree with, you can always interrupt to query."

Beatrice was suddenly moved by how mature her baby girl had suddenly become. As a matter of fact, she was so impressed with the changes in her youngest daughter ever since she had returned from what the family had come to term as her *sabbatical.* Val appeared to be a completely different person, someone who was willing to take on the world. Beatrice was indeed proud.

"So, Mum, remember that thing that happened to me when I was seven years old?"

Beatrice was very sure that this event would come up in their discussion. It is not one that she wished to speak about but drew strength from Val's composure and poise.

She said, "Yes, it is not something that a mother would soon forget."

Val continued, "I am not saying this to judge you or make you feel bad in anyway, but it is something that I have resolved to say as a part of the work that I have undertaken to ensure my healing. My therapist believes that my illness is not merely physical."

"What is it then? What else could it be?"

"I was getting to that."

"I'm sorry!"

"No, Mama, don't be! I am sorry for my tone. She believes that…"

"Your therapist is a girl!"

"Yes, Mama, and she is black."

"What? Black? Why would you see a black person? Wasn't there any white doctor who could help you?"

"Mama, please focus on what is important right now!"

"Well, I suppose she did help, so I guess she's alright!"

"Absolutely, Mama! I am a completely different person because of her!"

"Wow, that's different! Back in my day, certain jobs were reserved for just men and positively no blacks. Oh, how the world has changed!"

"I know, Mama! Society has come a far way. And I truly believe that you would really love her."

"Well, Val, love is a very strong word, but for all the changes I see in you which are directly related to your experience with her, I am grateful."

"Thanks, Mama. Well, what I wanted to say is, she believes and I have come to accept that my illness is not physical, its emotional. My headaches came as a result of extreme external stimulus which was overwhelming to my system; hence, it became toxic. It filled my body with so much toxicity that my body couldn't handle it so manifested this intolerance through a series of headaches. The main thing that triggered the headaches was resentment and I am sorry to say this but I have to. That resentment was directly related to you. I absolutely hated you."

Beatrice started to cry silently. By this, Val was crying as well. But now that she had said it, she was forced to continue, to say all that she came here to say.

"Yes, Mama, I am not proud of it. But I hated you. I hated you because I felt like you didn't love me enough, that you had abandoned me at a time when I needed you the most and this really hurt me, Mama. I felt like you had abandoned me just when I needed you the most. I felt like you had rejected me because I wasn't your perfect little girl anymore. And that really hurt me, Mama. So, for years I hated you! I couldn't stand to be in the same room with you."

Beatrice was weeping uncontrollably by this. They both were. It is a good thing that the poplar tree was somewhat secluded and offered them the seclusion that they needed. They held each other like they wouldn't let go. Eventually, Beatrice took control of the situation.

"I am terribly sorry that I made you feel that way. I truly am. But so many things were going on with you and I couldn't fix it. I am your mum and I am supposed to kiss you and make things better but I couldn't. And because I couldn't I felt weak, I was ashamed and I felt guilty. So, and I know this was wrong, but I felt helpless and helplessness gave way to hopelessness then apathy set in. I just decided that I preferred not to deal with anymore. I am so sorry, baby. I wish I could go back and do things different but I can't. I can only crave your forgiveness. Can you ever forgive me?"

"Of course, Mama! Just you saying that, means the world to me! That's all I ever wanted you to say, acknowledge my pain."

After that they made up. Things were not suddenly perfect between them, but it was amicable and everyone in the house was very happy for that because before Val left for her *sabbatical*, the tension was palpable. No one wanted to be around the two of them for too long because although no words were spoken, no words were ever spoken but the strain was very apparent in all their interactions. Gradually, they were both able to repair the breech, the first time in the history of the Whileys that such a thing was ever done. The first time, two Whileys had ever come together, acknowledged their misdeeds and worked in tandem to make amends. It was indeed, a tangible beautiful example for all the Whileys to learn from. Whether or not they learned was a different matter but a precedence had been established, an example for them to emulate and that was far more than any Whiley had ever accomplished. And somehow, that was enough.

Naturally, Val came to value her time spent in therapy and often used the various techniques she learned to counsel others. She would have gladly become a counsellor herself but was frequently warned that no Whiley (male or female) has ever worked for anyone except themselves. Unwillingly, she continued to keep all the books at Emersyn, isn't that what she had studied for? However, crunching numbers brought her absolutely no pleasure. Eventually, as their business dealings multiplied, she convinced her father to get her an assistant and a bigger staff so she played a more supervisory role in the accounting department of the Whiley business which by now had many business interests which needed to be accounted for.

****

All through dinner and indeed before, while we were touring Emersyn, I kept getting this feeling that I know this young man, Amoury. I get the distinct impression that we've met before. Maybe, because of his familiar green eyes that so many of us in my family have been blessed with. But it's not just that, it is his whole demeanour, his bearing. Now I understand Mason's reaction to him. Mason, who is always so stoic, in his response to strangers. Mason who is truly a Whiley in his thinking but has brought this black man to our ancestral home.

Even the Chloe incident left Amoury unfazed, it was as if he's been with us his whole life. It didn't even feel like we had a guest at dinner; believe it or not, he did not seem much perturbed at Everest and Andira's fussing, not in the least. In fact, no one but him seemed surprised when Mason invited him to stay the night. Could this be the change that Aunt Faith was talking about? This is a great change for us, no black person (male or female) has ever been invited to grace the walls of Emersyn. If Daddy were alive, he would have had an instant coronary, no wonder Mama is staying put in her room. I can't help but laugh at these sudden changes in the natural flow of our lives.

I was so excited that I so desperately wanted to speak with Mason but he looked so tired at dinner, I hate to disturb him. I guess I'll speak with him tomorrow. I'll just go check on Mum before going to bed. When I get there, I find Emery trying to communicate with her through a locked door trying to coax her to let him in.

He was saying, "Hi, Mama, it's Emery! Let me in! I just want to see that you're OK!"

He was met with complete silence. This is so typical Mama behaviour, when she doesn't get her way, she acts the fool. I joined him in trying to bring her out of her mood. But that was a dead end. So, we decided to leave her to her own devices. I ended up talking to Emery instead of Mason and I am happy I did because Emery and I have not had a chance to catch up in a long time. It is always refreshing talking to my brothers. I went to bed feeling so revived, so alive. What is going on with me?

Chapter Thirteen
A Knife Not a Wife

"I don't think anyone has a normal family." – Edward Furlong

Emery

Emery is the second of the Whiley children, a position that is unenviable because basically, in that position you're just a bystander. You watch things happen and you are powerless to initiate any real change. Luckily, Mason is not a despotic leader neither is he insecure nor is he apprehensive about his position as head of this family; because if he were any of those things, life could be way more difficult for Emery and indeed all his siblings. Also, luckily Mason did not marry a woman that was intemperate because that would be just as bad if not worse. In general, Mason is an extremely astute businessman; after all, that's the role he has been trained to play all his life but he is an absolutely phenomenal big brother. Mason makes sure to look out for everyone in this family equally and while growing up he has always been a friend and a confidant to Emery.

Emery has always been smaller than everyone in the family; even the girls are taller than him with or without heals. Something about not getting enough oxygen at birth. The truth is, Emery came a year after Mason and he was premature as his mum got critically ill during the pregnancy. She was in and out of the hospital and finally being as stubborn as she has always been, decided that if she were going to die, she would much prefer to die in the halls of magnificent Emersyn rather than some dismal and grimy hospital. She ended up experiencing a stroke which led to a mild heart attack and by the time they got her to the hospital – where she had to be airlifted to a much bigger facility – the baby was already in terrible distress. Emery was born at six months, two weeks, two days, had to be incubated for four months and weighed two and a half pounds at birth. This was devastating for Beatrice because she couldn't help feeling culpability for what had happened to her second child. Therefore, she always kept a closer eye on him, more than all the other children. In fairness to him, she felt like she owed him that much; seeing that she failed to take care of him in the womb. Everyone in the family came to accept Emery as their mum's favourite and everyone was OK with it; everyone that is, except Emery.

Emery perceived that being the only one singled out for cuddling in such a huge family; somehow, gave the appearance of being a weakling. The truth is even when Val was going through her gruesome ghost finding years, Mama did not offer Val any cuddling. Clearly not even Everest, who is the youngest among them got so much hand holding; just him, the pansy in the family. Elementary school was great but high school was an absolute nightmare. He was literally always in Mason's shadow. Emery was always Mason's little brother. Mason did not help much by being such a jock; captain for every striking thing he joined. Meanwhile, Emery could hardly swing a bat let alone catch a ball. It sucked even more because they look so much alike; same green eyes, same blonde hair same high cheekbones. High school was so horrible that Emery promised himself to get out from under Mason as he was being overshadowed and his accomplishments were eclipsed at every turn. Certainly, in his mind nothing he did could ever be as grand as Mason's effort.

Subsequently, Emery's childlike obsession with Mason's accomplishments led him to make some very poor decisions in his life. The irony is, every time he got himself into a predicament, it was always Mason who came to his rescue. For instance, when he was pretending to be a stud and got his girlfriend pregnant in college, it was Mason who came to his rescue. It was Mason's idea for them to have the baby and then put him up for adoption. It was Mason who convinced him that killing a child was the worst kind of murder. It was also Mason who somehow got them the money they needed to take care of his girl during the pregnancy. Good old Mason, always coming to his rescue. Now the issue is, he has a baby out their somewhere and he doesn't know where. Also, the fact that, his dad died without knowledge of his grandchild. One more thing for him to be obsessed with. Why couldn't he more like Mason? These things never happened to Mason who was always prudent; even Emery's wife had a crush on Mason and who could blame her.

Yes, Mason would always rush to his rescue but there was one situation that Mason was not able to rescue him from and that was marrying his wife, Amelia. For some reason, Emery had so programmed his own destruction that he ended up in a marriage designed to accomplish his demise. Unfortunately, it is the exact kind of situation that one could not share with anyone not even with his hero Mason; that would prove too embarrassing and would cause a terrible rift among the Whileys. Why didn't he just relent and listen to his parents? It is the exact type of circumstance that everyone in the family had warned him about so now he was too embarrassed to share it with anyone; he just had to suffer in silence, bear his burden alone. And indeed, for someone as sensitive as Emery, it was a huge load. A load that kept him awake at night; a just recompense for his defiance. Sometimes, he believed that the spirits of the Whileys long dead were active in punching him. If only Val could speak to them and get them to tell him how to get out of the mess he had gotten himself in.

Emery met and fell in love with Amelia a few months before he finished college and they dated for a really short time. Amelia is a few years older than Emery and made him feel like a strong, independent and autonomous individual. Initially, she saw him and treated him as an independent entity, separate from his family. Notwithstanding, the fundamental problem was that Emery had always been in love with Amelia but she was just along for the ride. At that time, she figured that at her age, she didn't have the right to be picky and figured she would get used to how needy he is. Over the years, being his mum's favourite had made him into the exact person that he really had no intentions of being.

Amelia did her research and realised that Emery came from money; old money. She wasn't too sure the magnitude of the inheritance but she wanted some of it for herself. Against the better judgement of his family, he got married to Amelia. Beatrice was at her wits end. She was sure and everyone agreed that Emery's marriage was going to be the death of her. The wedding was a really small affair, mostly Amelia's family because all the Whiley kids had been forbidden 'to set foot at that wedding'. Emery's siblings had really wanted to support him, but how could they go against the will of their parents? The powers that be; indeed the status quo, that is just not how things were done in their world. After the wedding, the big question on everyone's lips was where are they going to live? Beatrice was adamant that she would not live in the same house with that witch who has contrived this evil scheme and got her beloved son to go against her wishes. No, she would not stand for that scheming bitch to live in her house, that would be too much; adding insult to injury. In Beatrice's estimation, adding someone of the calibre as Amelia to their brood, would cause them to go from the sublime to the ridiculous. That would be way too much; what would people think of her family? They would think that they were losing their prestige. That really could not be allowed to happen.

Eventually, Cahal had to make the executive decision that Emery was a Whiley and by God that was never going to change; therefore, he would have to return home with his wife and live at Emersyn. That's just the way things are done in this family. No one is a cast away. Everyone is valued. That was also a wrong move because Amelia's family was dirt poor, she literally came from nothing and when she came to Emersyn, like so many others before her she was completely mesmerised by the grandeur that was Emersyn. To the point where she kept prodding Emery to usurp Mason, take control of the throne because Amelia dreamed of being mistress of Emersyn. At first, Amelia even tried to seduce Mason so that she could be queen but that did not work because Mason had too much integrity to allow that to happen. Plus Mason was so in love with Mauve that he would never do anything to jeopardise their relationship. It got so bad that Mason had to threaten Amelia with expulsion from Emersyn to get her to behave. That was the only thing that could put a halt to her pursuit because now that she has lived at Emersyn, she can't remember living anywhere else neither can she imagine living anywhere else.

The greatest heartbreak for Emery is the fact that, in all the years of generations living at Emersyn there has never been a Whiley who wants to conquer another Whiley to take the throne. All the Whileys follow the same rules, the same guidelines, which seems to be etched in their DNA. All the spouses came to adopt these principles, all of them, except Amelia. She clearly has not received that memo. Therefore, Emery is constantly on edge because Amelia is constantly plotting, constantly angry and miserable, constantly at odds with Mauve, who she sees as a real threat. Emery is in quite a fix, he is in complete misery because if Amelia were unhappy, no one would be happy, not him nor his two kids. Plus, the same Amelia, who use to treat him with love and respect, is the one who has become extremely disrespectful to him. This is the one thing that he has not been able to deny, her lack of respect for him.

That is the other issue perplexing poor Emery. They have three kids but one kid, the last one is definitely not his. The child looks nothing like any Whiley so ostensibly on one of his trips to the park, Emery took the baby to the doctor in a neighbouring community to get a DNA test done. Therefore, that is the other issue keeping him up at night. Also, unlike Everest and Andira who fight a lot,

Emery and his wife never fight, because they have to keep up appearances and protect their sham of a marriage.

Amelia keeps telling Emery, "You are thirty-seven years old and apart from that degree that you have, what have you accomplished?"

Mind you, Amelia does not have a degree. That was the other thing that almost drove Beatrice crazy. She ensured that all her children got a college education and here comes, her darling Emery, bringing home a wench who did not even have the ambition to finish high school (yes, she checked).

Unfortunately, that's the problem that Emery is now faced with, being married to someone who neither loves nor values him. He feels completely stuck and isolated. He is completely out of his depth in his current situation. Of late, he has been of the view that Val knows. Val who always knows, who knows more than she says and says even less than she knows. Previously, Emery tried to avoid Val, avoid her gaze because he just did not want to have that discussion with her or anyone else for that matter. But tonight, with Mama locked in her room, Mason inviting home a black guy and for sure Amelia was already plotting how she could use this to her advantage, Emery was just tired. Plus, having been an observer for such a long time, always looking for clues of his wife's unfaithfulness and while he did not have Val's gifting, there is something not right about their house guest; Amoury. He doesn't quite know what it is yet but as agreeable as he is, as handsome and articulate as he is, there is something off about him and Emery, for once feels strongly, that for the good of the cause he must say something. It is one thing to keep his private life a secret but another thing to keep something secret that could potentially affect all their lives. Also, it is quite alarming to him that Mason has not yet deduced that there is something unsettling about his house guest.

Yes, tonight, Emery feels compelled to act, to speak so he was very happy to get Val alone after dinner.

He told her, "Val, we have to talk."

Val responded, "Yes, I really need to talk to someone as well. Meet me in my room in fifteen minutes. I am going to check on Gabriel. He seemed really quiet at dinner."

With that they went their separate ways with plans to meet up later.

Chapter Fourteen
An Attack of Conscience

"These mountains that you are carrying, you were only supposed to climb." –
Najwa Zebian

Amoury

Life moves in leaps and bounds. Of all the places that I thought that I would end up, I would never have thought that I would be spending the night here at Emersyn. It seems so surreal, that after so many years of planning, after all the pain and suffering that a Cardinal has actually made his way into Emersyn and that Cardinal is me. I feel dazed like I am in a dream. The rain pounding on the roof is so rhythmic that it is the exact accompaniment required for this dreamlike moment. To many, the rain would be a damper but for me, I have always enjoyed the rain and saw it as a blessing, a cleanse, a purging of the Earth and my spirit. Plus, all the Whileys have been so cordial to me, I could hardly contain my guilt at dinner. It is good that none of them know me very well, or else they would have all been able to pinpoint my poker face.

I am seriously starting to question the viability my plan. Obviously, these are not the same people who brought harm to Laika. In all good conscience, I don't think they should be the ones to pay for a mistake that was made so many years ago. It would be the same as asking me to requite an injustice done by Laika himself. That just would not be very fair to me. Now I am here in this amazing house, in this wonderful bed but I can't sleep because my conscience won't let me. This is where I have desired to be for such a long time, based on Laika's story, where I have dreamed of being; yet I cannot enjoy the moment; oh, the irony.

Plus, it is noteworthy that their mum – Beatrice, yes that's her name – did not make an appearance at dinner. I know Mason said that she wasn't feeling well. But I can't help but wonder, if she is unwell because of me. I would hate to be responsible for the demise of an old woman who has never wronged me or my family. There was something quite telling in Mason's countenance when he returned from her room; all of a sudden, he looked quite exhausted. Not to mention, after his episode with Chloe. I couldn't help but laugh about that, Chloe falling in the toilet and squirming so much that the kids could not take her out. Poor Mason!

This family despite all appearances seems so normal. They could literally be my family at home in Beryl. Despite all the things that Laika has said about the Whileys and indeed others have said, I am starting to have a bad vibe about my own plan, my moral compass is beeping. It is somehow indicating that I should leave this house, abort my plans and forget everything I have ever heard about the Whileys and get on with my life.

But the other issue is Val. I really like her and when I leave here, I would at the very least try to keep in touch. I would also like to keep in touch with Mason as well. On the other hand, how can I leave now knowing that they will be in danger and that I am the one who has led this danger to them. Clearly, even if I abort my plan, the 'insider' is close enough to harm them so if I am not the instrument, someone else will be. Granted, it was not my idea but I am now a key player in this corrupt plan.

My phone is ringing; it must be my *associate* but what am I going to say! I can't tell him that I am out, he is likely to expose me and my deception revealed. That would invariably be worse. I better answer it.

"Hello."

"Hey, took you long enough to answer the phone."

"Sorry, I was in the bathroom."

"So how did today go?"

"It went well, better than I thought actually."

"Oh great! Are you back at the hotel? I could come by for an update."

"No, I'm at Emersyn."

"At Emersyn, you work really fast, I knew you were perfect for the job."

I genuinely cringe at this because I no longer want to be the best man for *the job* or any other job of this nature. I want to be well away from here, minding my own business and going to my classes. Even my politics class that I hate.

"Yes, I am here! Emersyn is way more magnificent than I ever imagined. She is overwhelming."

Yes, stall with small talk.

"Yes, that's exactly why my boss wants to take it back."

"Wait, hold on! You mean the insider, don't you?"

"Well… yeah… him too, not just him, my boss."

"Which boss? You never told me that you had a boss before. This changes everything, I thought we shared the same motives, the same agenda. Now I come to hear that you have a boss! I didn't know that there are other people involved. So, who exactly is your boss?"

He says sheepishly, "Well, I don't know exactly, we have never met. I just wait for his instructions using a burner phone that I received in the mail."

"A burner phone? Wait for instructions? A boss you have never met?"

I realise that I am on the verge of shouting so I lock myself in the ample bathroom.

"When were you going to tell me all this? That you are merely a puppet in this operation? How can I trust you or him, someone you have never met?"

"Don't call me that! I am not a puppet. I hate when people say that about me! I wasn't even supposed to tell you, it just slipped, so forget that I said anything."

"Look, man, I am out! This is too much for me! I didn't sign up for this! I don't even know what your boss is capable of."

"You can't just be out. My boss will definitely be angry and he will not allow that. There is no place in this plan to press the abort button. Too bad that you have suddenly grown a conscience."

"Oh wow! I have to go! I need time to think."

I hang up my phone, while he is saying, "We are both in too deep—"

I can't help but wonder aloud, "What in tarnation have I gotten myself involved in."

Now that some unknown entity is involved, I absolutely need to take action. I think I need to remove myself from this equation. I can't tell Mason; especially, now that I know that someone potentially more duplicitous is involved. Or can I? And just let the chips fall where they may? I swear that if Emersyn wasn't so far away from everything, I swear that I would just call an Uber and get the hell out of here. But how can I just leave when I have unleashed this hell on them that will potentially disrupt the natural order of their life forever? Plus, I cannot leave Val in danger, that would be inhumane.

Well, I am going to sleep on this and when I wake up in the morning I will go according to my first inclination. So thankful for the rain and the mountains so near.

Please come to me sweet sleep. Sleep is hard when your heart and head are at war but eventually she comes in ebb and flowing motions which always leaves me drained in the morning.

Chapter Fifteen
Chronicles of the Third Child

"Hoping for the best, prepared for the worst, and unsurprised by anything in between." – Maya Angelou

Gabriel

Gabriel is four years younger than Mason and three years younger than Emery. In the grand scheme of things that does not seem like a long time but it was long enough for him to feel alienated from his older brothers. Gabriel always felt like a third wheel whenever he was around his brothers. He always felt like they somehow had a secret code and they were in cahoots about something and had planned to keep him out of the loop. The problem was sometimes they would share an innocent joke but Gabe would just be off the opinion that they were laughing at him. In truth, he presumed that everyone in the family was laughing at him; even his parents.

Gabe as he is affectionately called, is the third child and third son in the Whiley family. Gabe is very melancholy by nature, he has always been this way, as far back as when he was a baby. Through elementary he was a loner, he engaged in none of the frolicking with kids his age. I guess it was in elementary school where his path had been set. In high school, he still lacked all the mirth of youth. Generally, he just seemed like a very miserable old man. Beatrice often joked to Cahal that Acram Whiley had been reincarnated in their son. Cahal would just take that at face value and saw it for the humour that it conveyed but sometimes in watching her son, Beatrice was genuinely afraid that something might be seriously wrong with her child.

Gabriel had come to be suspicious of everything that was happening around him. It didn't help that when he went to college, his first week, he was attacked and robbed at gun point by a masked gunman. The police never made an arrest. Therefore, he spent his entire college years looking out for the next person who would mug him, the one who would destroy him; that incident really changed him at his core. He became even more reserved and made very little attempts to make friends.

In a big family, everyone is generally known for something. Gabriel is known for two things, for being a cynic and a writer. Of course, he had never published anything and indeed wouldn't because he did not feel like anyone outside his immediate family would appreciate his work. Even within his own family, he thought that they were just being gracious to him. He felt like deep down they did not have a full understanding of his work. And why should they when his work was always so dark. At college, his professors encouraged him to write but just less dark material. They encouraged him to write about happier things, things befitting his youth. But the one thing that these experiences created in him was a deep sense of being a realist. He was never in denial about a situation, he could always tell when he was being deceived.

Compounded by the fact that, his demeanour was generally frail, ill-humoured; naturally, he had very few friends so much so that when he informed his family of his pending wedding everyone was shocked. Her name was Alison and when he brought her to Emersyn, everyone kept looking for signs that indicated a lopsided connection but there wasn't any. Beatrice was totally blown away by her beauty, candour and humour. She kept asking Cahal if he thinks it's a trick and she just wanted Gabe for the money. Why else would such a vision want to be tied to a scrooch? Cahal said, 'Have faith, Beatrice, we've been good people so just accept that God is showing us favour by way of a great wife for our worse kid.' Needless to say, Beatrice was not amused. Everyone in the family was anxious to meet his bride and went out of their way to be extremely kind to her lest she changed her mind. Also, they all felt deep down that she was merely taking one for the team. But they couldn't believe how stunning and jovial Alison was. All they could conclude was that opposites really and truly attract. How else could they explain it?

Surprisingly, through Alison's soothing influence, she actually made Gabe far more pleasant than he had ever been. They were extremely happy together, even the blind could see that. Consequently, they were always the centre of attention – discretion has never been the Whiley's strong suit – as everyone kept looking for signs of distress in their marriage. For instance, some sort of SOS from the new bride but none was forthcoming. Gabe's sibling would often bump into each other outside his door listening for anguished voices. 'Oh, excuse me!

Fancy meeting you here,' became an inside joke for the Whiley kids, a running gaff, which spoke to the complete lack of faith that they had in Gabe. All this attention was really disturbing for Gabe, who had endeavoured to live his life outside of the limelight. But in spite of that, he really blossomed into a better version of himself and everyone loved seeing him bloom. Gradually, everyone breathed a huge sigh of relief and realised that they could stop worrying about Gabe and Alison as they both seemed to be in it for the long haul.

Gabriel had been married for three glorious years and they had one child, Gabriella, but sadly their child passed away and her mum was unable to take the strain, so she took her own life. He sometimes wished that Val could get in touch with them so he would know that they are doing well. But they had come to realise that Val's gift did not exactly work like that. Despite her name in high school, she didn't exactly find the ghosts, on the contrary, they usually find her. In the meanwhile, Gabriel just decided to accept his lot in life, being a realist, he harboured no fantasy of anything better happening for him. Although he never stopped mourning for his beautiful wife and the life they could have had. He often turned to his dark writings in times of storm. However, tonight nothing could comfort him as he felt really agitated as if something untoward was about to happen. He had learned to trust this feeling, trust his instinct because this is exactly how he felt the week when his baby was going to die and later when his wife took her own life. It really hadn't helped that Mason had brought home a stranger. What if this man was somehow here to kill them in their sleep? He literally jumped when he heard the knock on the door and was extremely relieved when he realised that it was just Val, his younger sister.

"Hey, Val, why are you still up?"

"I could ask the same of you, little bro."

We both laugh at that. She loves to do that. Turn my question into her statement. Apparently, she was on a mission and she was going to budge so I let her in. She said, 'I just came to check on you. You did not seem so perky at dinner.' That moved him more than she knew, more than he would let her know. The fact that so many people were at dinner and Val took the time to enquire about him. That was the other thing about Val (apart from her ghost finding skills) she was very good at reading people and sometimes it even seemed like she was feeling exactly how he was feeling. At times it felt like her very presence, took some of the burden, like she was helping him, carry some of the load.

113

Normally, Gabriel is so very secretive and he always kept his thoughts until he had worked through the cracks in them; however, tonight he felt moved to share those thoughts with Val. Val, who had left everyone else in the house and came to see about him. Something not even his mum has done in a long time. Sure, after the funerals, they all piled in his room but gradually they came less and less and these days, not at all. To be fair to Mason, he did try his best to reach out to Gabe but Gabe generally took every opportunity to stay in his room and in his head.

Chapter Sixteen
The Bad Seed

"Children must be taught how to think, not what to think." – Margaret Mead.

Valen Finley

Valen is the great, great, great, great, great, great, great grandson of Rance Tillerman. The same Tillerman who had lost his most prized possession to Whiley in a card game. Valen was the son of Tillerman's granddaughter Emma Jade. Emma Jade's dad Phin was the youngest child for Rance Tillerman. Phin was married to Adalynn. Adalynn was not from Shrove; she was from a few communities away. She was the second daughter of a poor farmer who had passed away in his prime and wasn't prudent; therefore, he did not leave an inheritance for his family so that left Adalynn's mum Ida to do everything for their six children. Life was hard for Ida and that made her bitter.

Phin by no means could be described as a go getter neither could he be described as an individual who takes initiative. He greatly depended on his father and his older siblings to make decisions for him. Later, when he married Adalynn she made most of the decisions for their little family. Therefore, when Tillerman lost most of his investments, things made became really difficult for a young man who hadn't learned to flex his own muscles, who relied heavily on his family for support. Adalynn was more enterprising but at a time when opportunities for women were limited and male dominance was the order of the day; her hands were tied pretty tight. She had to rely heavily on her husband's decisions or indecisions, whatever the case maybe.

Emma was the youngest of Rance's five grandchildren so she did not understand until later in life what had happened and why she had to leave her beautiful room in their mansion to live in a hovel. Because really, everywhere else compared to Emersyn is a shed. As usual, no one thought of explaining things properly to the children so they were left to put the bits and pieces together, to formulate their own opinions on events that were critical to their well-being.

Rance was in no way a wealthy man, he had made a few investments, some paid off others didn't. The little wealth came from cotton. He was in no way as astute as Acram Whiley. He didn't understand money, he didn't quite understand the power in diversifying, neither was he as good as Acram at assessing a situation and identifying an opportunity. At the time, he wasn't thinking about a legacy or the fact that his father had set him up financially for life. It was a case of easy come, easy go. As is the way of the human condition, he only arrived at that awareness after his recklessness had cost him something so immense and important to his bloodline that money couldn't buy. Hence, the reason, he would have put himself in such a position to lose Emersyn.

After Rance had lost Emersyn, he became a shell of his former self. He drank more, was seriously ill-tempered and reticent when he was sober. His family thought that losing his connection to Emersyn had driven him crazy as he was often confused and seen conversing with himself. Really, who could blame the man? Emersyn had been in his family for years. In fact, she had been designed and constructed by his great, great grandfather so he was destined to go down in history as the nincompoop who ended their rich heritage. That was too much for anyone to bear. He tried reasoning with Whiley, then beseeching, later bribing but nothing worked. Because one thing with that Acram, he knew a good thing when he saw it and definitely this was the best thing that ever happened to hm. Rance explained to him that this was surely going to wreck his family, destroy his name but Acram didn't care. He merely mocked and ridiculed him for his bad luck.

Tillerman had no choice but to move the family into a smaller and newer house but it was not Emersyn and Rance's drinking meant that less money was being spent in the house. His grown children tried to reason with him, suggest other options but he had lost his drive and with that the will to live; especially, after he had come to see all the things Acram had accomplished. Also, he spent less time focusing on the business ventures that he had left. Consequently, they had to move a few more times and every time they moved Rance became even more bitter and resentful. It was painful to watch the gradual decline of a great man. Eventually, Rance ended even more withdrawn; when all is said and done, drinking himself to death. Many of his supporters gave credence to the idea that he died of a broken heart.

Not unexpectedly, it broke his family's heart to see the tragic demise of their patriarch; going from the sublime to the ridiculed. In the end, he was unrecognisable even to himself and as always in times of grief, the human mind swings inward, examining itself. There is a great desire to know why. The why is often far more complex than anyone is willing to admit. Definitely, the mind will select the most obvious and certainly the most convenient rejoinder. In this tragic and painful situation, Whiley and his clan were the most obvious culprits. It goes without saying that they were easy to hate, hold accountable; hence, damnable. Accordingly, all the hurt, pain and blame was laid squarely at the Whiley's gate. The framework was therefore set, which set plans into motion for the ultimate destruction of the Whiley name; just a total erasure of their existence.

Life was pretty confusing for Emma Jade after they were forced to leave Emersyn. It wasn't even so much the fact that they had to leave but it was the abruptness of the transaction. The suddenness which didn't give anyone enough time to process what had happened. Also, the problem was her dad – Phin like all his siblings – had been employed to Tillerman Inc. but now all that had been lost. For a long time, Phin was really angry with his dad but gradually he came to be angrier with Acram and ultimately with himself. He despised the fact that he couldn't find the vigour or the unction to function. To that end, Phin was caught between two opinions; on the one hand, he felt like he had the rugged pulled out from under him while on the other, he was expecting any day now for someone to say it was all a hoax and then he would have gotten his old life back. Needless to say; he envied his siblings for their swift recovery and natural tendency towards spontaneity, when he was still trying to find the rug, which he felt might have given him a bit of stability until he was able to find his footing.

Phin's anger was unleashed on his wife, Adalynn, who had always been a nag and now she was worse because deep in her heart, she harboured a fear of returning to her mummy's house. Adalynn had never gotten along with her mum and when she got married to Phin Tillerman, their relationship deteriorated even more, since her mum nursed animosity towards her as she was jealous that Adalynn had fared better in marriage than she had. Every time, Adalynn tried to aid her family, Ida was of the view that Adalynn was flaunting her new found wealth in her face.

The pressure of their new life, the moving, the general lack of mirth in their life caused Phin and Adalynn to fight all the time. Some of these fights got pretty violent and each time, Adalynn convinced herself that this was the last time. Eventually, the sheriff had to be called and she spent a night at the local hospital. At the time, going to a hospital was a novelty as most people preferred to endure their pain and suffering at home, but everyone including the sheriff agreed that she was in a really bad way so she needed to see a doctor. Clearly, they were right, as she suffered a concussion, a broken rib and a broken collar bone. But of course, no arrest was made because it was plain to see that, this was both a domestic affair and an unfortunate misunderstanding. She knew it was time to leave. Sadly, little Emma Jade was privy to all this unpleasantness which left an ineffaceable impression on her. As kids often do, at first, she blamed herself but later she got a better understanding of who was culpable in this situation.

Gradually, Phin and Adalynn's relationship deteriorated to the point of no return because of all the Tillerman's children, their relationship suffered the most irreparable damage. There was just too much water under the bridge. Apparently, their entire relationship was built around the presence of Emersyn in their life and clearly without that they had nothing in their lives. Or quite possibly they were too young and immature to weather the proverbial storm. Invariably, they filed for a divorce and little Emma had to leave Shrove to live away from her dad with her mum as her mum returned to her family home. She had to leave all her friends, all her cousins and most of her beloved dolls and pretty dresses. Mummy had said there was no room where they were going.

While it was fun living there, because there were so many people at the house; including kids her age, it was a very crowded place all the time. There was absolutely no privacy. Plus, her mum seemed to always be in conflicts with her own mother, which is easy to see why because her mum didn't have a job so she was always available for a spat with her mum. They mostly farmed and Adalynn had decided that farming was not her thing. Consequently, she was in one miserable relationship after the next trying to recreate what initially she had with Phin. However, one man after the next was a disappointment because a huge part of Phin's attraction was the fact that he came with Emersyn.

Emma only saw her dad and her beloved grandfather on holidays. On one of those holidays when she returned home, she discovered that her grandfather had died. Jade was completely devastated. Suddenly, her world made absolutely no sense. How could her grandpa be gone forever? She didn't quite understand but every time she asked what happened the name Whiley kept coming up. No one really took the time to explain the situation accurately to Emma; therefore, she grew up hating the name Whiley. She hated them based on everything that the adults had said.

Later, when she was in her late teens, she returned to Shrove, again made the discovery that her absolutely most favourite cousin Quentin had been murdered by the Whiley boys. They weren't sure which one and somehow they had been released on a technicality. She was livid. First, they take her home, her life, her grandfather and then the life of her favourite cousin. It seemed like, everything that went wrong in her life was somehow attached to the Whiley name. This time they had gone too far. Something had to be done. From that moment she started plotting revenge, she had indeed set the ground work because whatever she had not been able to accomplish in her life time, she left very clear and specific instructions, by way of malice towards the Whileys which were passed down from generation to generation ensuring the ultimate destruction of the Whileys. To make them pay for all the hell they had rained down on her family.

Just like Laika's family, many had tried and now it was Valen's turn. However, Valen was not the smartest apple on the tree. He hadn't finished high school and had come to visual all the ills in his life as a by-product of the Whiley wickedness – as the old adage goes, *children live what they learn and learn what they live.* They absolutely had to be punished for all the wrongs that they had inflicted on his family.

Valen's parents' marriage had ended in divorce and he is the only child for both of them. They are very hardworking people and that is the only reason they got a divorce; they worked too hard, they worked odd hours, they had simply grown apart because they had been able to grow together as a result of their work situation. After the divorce, Valen had opted to live his mum as his dad was never home. His mum worked better hours and was also very laidback but his dad was a stickler and would have insisted that he cleaned his room and do his homework. Also, his dad would have insisted that he dropped some of those friends that he had started hanging out with. While Valen had a very good childhood and despite being divorced, parents who loved him and just wanted the very best for him, he had decided at a young age that he wanted things quick and easy. Therefore, he found all his classes tedious, his dad even offered to get him a tutor, but that would not do for him because regardless, a tutor would still make him do work.

Unsurprisingly, Valen had dropped out of high school to invest in other more substantive business with his friends who were much older than him. As a consequence, he was known to the police that he had spent some time in the county jail. As a consequence, of his less than desirable reputation with law enforcement, Valen made the decision to return to Shrove – having spent his whole life hearing about Shrove – after he left high school. He bounced about the town for a while, doing odd jobs, just trying to stay under the radar, but he couldn't find a footing. At first, he spent much of his days surveilling Emersyn from a distance because apart from the fact that Emersyn had a huge gate a few miles from the front door, Cahal had invested in a very expensive security system, until eventually he had become obsessed with her as much as many others before.

Valen had imagined himself so many times just living in Emersyn – compounded by the illegal substances that he enjoyed so much – he became obsessed with Emersyn, to the point where he was having illusions of grandeur that he actually started to believe that Emersyn was rightfully his and now that he had seen it first-hand he knew for sure that he had to own it.

Some people are accident prone, while others are trouble prone. Valen is the type of person who can find trouble even in a grave yard. He was always mixing with the wrong crowd; he never did learn how to choose his friends wisely or it was more a case where he just allowed himself to be chosen. Everybody was his friend. He therefore took no active part in the choosing because the thing about people who have been chosen is that sometimes they forget that at some point they have to also chose for themselves instead of just rolling with the tide.

Unsurprisingly, again based on Valen's track record, things came to ahead when he got into trouble with some really bad people and had promised them payment based on the fact that Emersyn belonged to his family and they were going to sell it so he would pay them from his share. Of course, he didn't tell them this because everyone for miles around knew that the Whileys owned Emersyn and the younger generations knew nothing about the Tillermans in relation to Emersyn. The Tillermans had come to be known as a very hardworking, respectable family so Valen was an abrasion on the Tillerman name.

As might be expected, after watching the house for a while, seeing who lived there, who went in and out, he came up with a plan. A wildcard, but desperate times require even more desperate measures.

Chapter Seventeen
When It Rains, It Pours

"Half my life is an act of revision." – John Irving

Amoury

Generally, I love to wake up early and to witness the sunrise especially in this bucolic setting. The sunrise is always so inspiring as it highlights and celebrates the possibilities of a brand-new day. It wasn't always like this for me though because I am a city boy; hence, I was never a fan of seeing the sunrise or even the sunset or anything scarcely related to nature. In fact, I really and thoroughly enjoy city life, the accessibility of everything. However, all that changed for me once I started studying anthropology with a specific focus on both visual anthropology and archaeology and after my school trip to South Africa.

On our trip we stayed in a little village just outside Johannesburg where the air is consistently fresh and clean in the countryside. South Africa is home to the most picturesque sunrise and sunset that I have been privy to; also, the richness of the landmass is an anthropologist's dream. We visited Robben Island where the great orator Nelson Mandela was held captive but now it is home to one the finest museums that side of the Atlantic. Robben Island is located in Table Mountain which overlooks Cape Town, my classmates and I actually hiked to the top; the view is mind blowing, like nothing I had ever seen before or since. Table Mountain is an awe-inspiring natural phenomenon, one of the most amazing in the world with flora and fauna endemic only to that region. An absolute gem of nature. I am sure this is where my fondness for mountains come from.

As might be expected, in the city where I live, it is extremely difficult to observe aspects of nature with so much artificial lighting everywhere. Initially, our home, Beryl, was outside the city limits but by the time the developers started building around us, we were smack in the heart of the city. None of us wanted to leave because this house had been in our family long before Laika met the Cardinals. I guess deep down, I am a country boy at heart.

I woke up with a splitting headache. It was still early in the morning. I had slept with my curtains open, so I could tell that the sun was just coming up over the horizon and the rain had stopped. As a matter of fact, despite the luxury I was in, I did not get a good night's sleep. I kept tossing, turning and thinking about what needed to be. In fact, I only woke up because of the noise outside my door. I went to enquire and Mason was standing there surrounded by what appears to be all their children combined – the next generation of Whileys. Apparently, there was a problem with Chloe again.

Mason was saying, "Well, how do you know that she is missing?"

A small girl with piercing blue eyes said, "We checked all her favourite places."

A tall boy, resembling Mason joins in.

"Yes, we checked the kitchen, behind the fridge, behind the curtains in the foyer, the hallway outside grandma Beatrice's room. She's just nowhere to be found."

A girl, with the hair colour of corn being harvested, adds, "Yes, MJ is right, me, Marla, Cass and Ethan all double checked all the usual places where she usually hides and we think maybe she probably got caught in the rain, so she might be outside, soaking wet daddy. You have to find her!"

Mason was saying, "OK, Marigold, don't worry."

All the kids suddenly joined in chanting, "Please find her! You've gotta find her!"

Some holding him by his hands, the really small ones, his legs.

Mason looked so concerned. He managed to take control of the situation and told the kids, "Don't worry! Leave this to the grown-ups. Go have breakfast. We'll sort out this Chloe mess."

That seems to pacify them. Seemingly, accustomed to Mason keeping his word.

I get dressed quickly, endeavouring to help. It's the least that I could do.

While I was getting ready, I weighed my options; tell Mason about my duplicitous plan or not and continue to associate with potential criminals or not. While I was brushing my teeth, I looked at myself in the mirror, like a really judicious look and asked myself some really serious questions. Is this the legacy that I want to leave behind? Would Laika want to bring down the Whileys so badly that he would be involved with thieves and robbers and God knows who else? Would Laika risk his life to exact vengeance? Could I live with myself if any harm came to any of these innocent children? Why can't we all just get along?

By the time I had gotten dressed, the sun was already up. As I reflect on the conversation that Mason had with the kids, I cannot imagine a villain being so concerned about a cat; especially, one as prone to mischief as this one seems to be. Based on Mason's instructions, we are going out to search for her, with the mandate that we have to find her at all costs or he would indeed be in deep hot water with the kids. He had promised and his word was his bond.

As I stepped outside with the others, I am hit by the crisp morning air. The air feels so clean and fresh, almost as if it had been filtered, as always, my mind goes back to my conundrum and I asked myself, after this, could I ever be clean again? Could I ever return from this? Is this a story that I would be proud to tell my kids? Now I understand how Hamlet felt in his unique predicament when he was so moved to utter, *"How all occasions inform against me, and spur my dull revenge."* However, in my case, I am being spurred *against* the act of vengeance. For the first time since I came up with this scheme, I have to consider the theory of the ripple effect. I am face to face with how many real people are going to get hurt. Doesn't the good book also say, *Beloved, never avenge yourselves, but leave it to the wrath of God, for it is written, 'Vengeance is mine, I will repay,' says the Lord.*

I now know exactly what I had to do. I had to give Mason the heads up after we took care of this Chloe business. But I have to get him alone first which is going to prove more difficult than I care to admit.

****

Val

It was great chatting with my brothers last night but somehow the subject matter left me unsettled. Both Emery and Gabe are of the opinion that despite Amoury's affable demeanour and obvious intelligence, Mason is undeniably making a mistake going into business with this man. Emery says, he smells fishy while Gabe believes that he smells like a rat. I am quite surprised because these two are always stuck in their head, seeming like the Titan Atlas, to be carrying the world on their head. I strongly disagree with their appraisal. I just get a different vibe about him, I can't exactly put my finger on what it is but I trust him. Where they see deceit, I see quiet confidence and mild amusement. Also, my brothers have lived in such absolute seclusion all their lives that I think they are more concerned about the fact that Amoury looks different; hence, the notion that he might be a danger to any of us. We have been so programmed by society to see the other as bad, never good, never something to embrace unquestioningly.

I really need to speak with Mason privately before anyone else gets to him. But first we have to take care of this Chloe problem.

****

Mason

On a normal day, I love to wake up early and observe the sunrise but today, I woke up with a throbbing headache. I thought a goodnight sleep, with the pitter patter of the soothing raindrops against the window and the roof that my headache would have cleared, but nope. Mauve believes that I am overthinking and this is the source of my headache. But of course, I am thinking too much, I am the one responsible for all the major decisions in this family so if I mess up, it's not just me and my family that's affected. My siblings and mum will be greatly impacted but also all the over three hundred employees who work for us, in one capacity or the next. Now I understand what my dad meant when he used to say with a sigh, *heavy is the head that wears the crown.*

As soon as I woke up, I remembered my dilemma with Mama. I wish I could have just stayed asleep. Just when I was thinking of sleeping in for an extra hour, here comes the kids again, another Chloe problem. Apparently, they've looked everywhere for her and she cannot be found. Maybe, I should have listened to my siblings and flush Chloe last night.

So, I get up quickly, get three search parties together. I keep Amoury with me, along with the twins, Amethyst and Melisandre. Emery, Gabe and Val are together while Everest, Andira and Amelia are all the same group. They are all miserable alike, they deserve each other. Some of us will have to go towards the gate, others will go towards the mountain and others will just check the property.

****

Amoury

This mountain is nothing compared to Table Mountain, but it is indeed formidable; a challenge in its own right. I was really hoping for a few minutes alone with Mason but that's not going to happen with his twin siblings so near. They are really quiet; they don't say much at all. Most of the discussion is initiated by Mason. Personally, I am OK with silence; especially, since I have so much on my mind. Apart from Val and obviously Mason, I am not entirely sure who can be trusted among the Whiley clan. Thankfully, when we are half way up the hill, Mason gets a call, something about his mum and it being urgent. There was a lot of static on the line so, Mason didn't hear the message too clearly.

After he disconnects, he says, "What now!"

The twins almost simultaneously say, "Just Mum being Mum!"

Melisandre rolls her eyes. Amethyst quickens his pace as if he couldn't care less.

Mason declares, "If you guys want to continue, that's fine but I have to get back to the house to see what's happening."

Melisandre says, "I'll continue searching with Amethyst. If there's no sign of Chloe in an hour we'll turn back."

I decide to return with Mason, happy for the time alone with him finally. We turn to go to the twins simultaneously calling, 'CHLOE! CHLOE! CHLOE!' and Amethyst saying, 'Get your butt home, Chloe! I'm going to skin you alive for this nonsense. This is a grand waste of my valuable time; you, mutt.'

Mason grins. 'He's all heart, that Amethyst.' We both laugh at his attempt at humour despite the strain.

On our way down, we talk about our families. I tell him about my two siblings, my parents and that my dad had died recently. At that, he was sympathetic seeing that he had lost his dad recently as well. After a few minutes of silence, he said, "Sometimes, I wish my dad was still alive, then all this mess would be his worry." I remain silent, what I am I going to say. I wish he hadn't confided that. Now I feel so much worse.

After more pauses, Mason, narrates the story of how Shrove was founded. He tells me the story of the Whileys from Acram to his dad. He informs me about a great, great, great grand uncle, Lawrence, who had lost his mind after returning from the Civil War and had disappeared without a trace. The family still don't have a clue what had happened to Lawrence. One thing about the Whileys, they keep a clear account of their history at their fingertips. He tells me how he met his wife. I tell him that I have not had any time for romance, with my studies and all. That is part of the truth but the plain truth is that, I have been planning my attack on the Whileys, too focused for a relationship. Apart from my university days, this is the first time I can actually say that I've shared a moment with a friend. O, share that with him and he blushes.

Soon we are talking again, he asks me about my usual green eyes.

I asked him, "You mean to ask, how did a black guy end up with eyes like yours?"

He stops and looks at me, blushes again and then laugh a mischievous laugh. A laugh that I like. A laugh that colours him human. I go on tell him more about my family, the Cardinal side. I don't say anything about Laika, lest there is a record of him in their family. Surprisingly, I am enjoying our talk, it doesn't feel weird anymore. Just like I thought, Mason is a genuinely nice guy.

All this time, in our tête-à-tête, I am waiting on an opportune juncture, an opening to say what I have to say. Because really what I have to say, cannot be rushed and I really need to the right segue, the right moment to broach this topic. How am I supposed to tell a man who has taken me in his confidence that I'm just here to destroy everything him and his family has worked for all their lives.

I am so deep in thought about my own troubles, I am pretty sure I have missed some of what he has just said. I am brought back to the present when I see him stop abruptly and he pauses with a look of horror on his face. I think, in my reverie I probably said something stupid without realising it. I quickly scan my brain to see if I allowed anything to leak out. But then I notice that he has his phone in his hands. Then it dawns on me that I didn't say anything stupid; in fact, I didn't say anything at all. I so relieved, I could cry.

That joy is short lived because he says, "Quick! We have to get back to the house! Mama is sick!"

I take off running, trying to catch up with him, while trying to ascertain what had happened but he's too fast. I cannot keep up with him. Who knew such a tall guy could run so fast? What am I saying? Mason is just as tall as Usain Bolt, the fastest man alive. I decide to just take my time, there is no way I can catch up to him. I wonder what could have happened. And like the old adage, *a guilty conscience needs no accuser;* because immediately, I start to wonder if Mason's mum somehow got wind of my plan and she died. Or is she waiting there with the police?

When I finally got to the house, I wish she had been waiting there with the police.

Chapter Eighteen
Disruptions and Disturbances

"Not all storms come to disrupt your life, some come to clear your path." –
Anonymous

Mason

I get home and really wished I had stayed in bed all day.

There are police officers, fire fighters and paramedics all over my living room. We have not had so many visitors to the house since the days of my mum's extravagant parties. Unfortunately, Mama is not dressed in her finest, definitely not looking her best. Everyone is trying to talk to me at once. The paramedics are saying her blood pressure is so high she probably had a stroke. The police officers are saying something about a bone. They say they wanted to speak with me down by the station. I told them that I have to attend to my mum and I will come down as soon as possible.

The senior detective said, "This is not urgent but we'd like to speak to you as soon as possible."

So, I said, "What is this about?"

He said, "Quite possibly about a cold case."

"A cold case? What do you mean?"

He said, "A lot is going on right now. We'll speak to you, when you get some time."

With that the police officers left. In all the years, the Whileys have lived at Emersyn, we have never had law enforcement traipsing around, tracking mud everywhere. The paramedics stowed Mama in the ambulance, Val was with her. They told me that I could meet them at the hospital. Mum is going to the hospital; a place she loathes. How could this have happened? Mauve says she'll go with me and explain this issue in the car. Mauve spins the weirdest tale, I've ever heard in a long time.

Mum had finally relented and opened her door to the prodding of the servants. She was having breakfast when Chloe returned from her escapades. Heaven knows where Chloe had been all night. While everyone was out looking for her, she came back on her own. Apparently, she was not alone. She had brought back a bone. A human bone. As usual, she loves to provoke mum, so she decided to bring the bone to mum's room; evidently, to share her find. Mum took one look at the bone, let out an ear-piercing scream and fainted. Now they are trying to figure out if she hit her head when she fell.

I was almost at the hospital when I remembered the twins. I reached for my phone to call Amethyst. Once I parked I realised that he had called me over twenty times. I thought possibly he had heard about Mama and was just worried so he was calling to get more details. He answers on the first ring.

"I've been trying to reach you for the last twenty minutes."

He almost yelled.

So, I said, "Calm down, Mama is at the hospital."

He said, "What? Mum is at the hospital?"

By now he was definitely yelling.

Now I was really, concerned.

"So, if you weren't calling me about Mum, why were you calling me so many times?"

He said something I never thought I'd heard, "Mel is missing, Mason!"

I said, "WHAT?"

He said, "We got separated on the mountain and I called her cell, I've been yelling out her name and I've not heard from her, not a peep."

"Omg! What is happening today?"

Mauve was saying something but I don't know what she's saying. I think I tell her because now she's screaming. I tell her to remain calm.

I tell Amethyst, "Go home and call the police."

In less than an hour the police would have been at our house twice. The same ones probably will just turn around and return to the house.

So many various disruptions and disturbances in one day. What else could possibly go wrong today?

Part Two

Chapter Nineteen
The Twins

"Oh, what a tangled web we weave… when first we practise to deceive." –
Walter Scott

Melisandre

The twins are fraternal, and they couldn't be more alike but that being said, they are also quite different; because where Amethyst is cold and unyielding Melisandre is warm and considerate. Mel is quite similar to Val in many ways and is always conflicted about her role in the family because while Mel is the older sister; Val is seen as the go to sister while, Mel is just the beautiful one who seems to lack a sense of drive and purpose. But again, while Mel lacks these attributes, Amethyst – or Thyst as Mel calls him, who by the way is the only one allowed to call him this – has them in an abundance.

Clearly, they seem in some uncanny way to complete each other's persona. Amethyst undoubtedly being the evil twin and Val his benevolent alter ego. That being said, they are as thick as thieves as they bring balance to each other and seem to need each other to survive. It would appear that one would break in a million pieces if deprived of the others presence.

Now Mel is so sweet which makes her both susceptible and vulnerable to Thyst's manipulation. Of course, she was always aware when he was exploiting her but she always went along with it as she loved him unconditionally and trusted him unreservedly. She has always felt that she needed him more than he needed her. Amethyst doesn't really need anyone; he doesn't even act like he wants his wife; half the time she is off travelling the world with their three children. Also, while Mel is fiercely intelligent her mum has always warned her against being such a *Ms Smarty Pants*, since men had no place in their lives for a woman who is smarter than them. Therefore, over the years, Mel has learned to temper her ambitions, deprecate her value in the world and to her huge family.

In fact, a few years ago, she was in love with a local boy, Timothy Sanderson who she went to high school with and her parents simultaneously talked her out of marrying him despite the fact that she was head over heels in love with him and he with her. Intuitively she knew that they would have a great life. But even while she was spending time with him, she knew that her father would probably kill her with his bare hands and her mum would hold her in place before they gave their blessings. Eventually, she succumbed to their pressure and broke her heart by breaking his. She knew it had to be done and it was the only way to protect Timothy because of her parents willing to murder her, imagine what they would have done to him. Sometimes Mel wished that she were more like Val, strong willed and resolute in her resolve not to marry.

Eventually, Mel had married a man that was hand-picked by her parents; Nolan of the Mathison clan, who loved her unwaveringly yet she could not love him because her heart belonged to Timothy. In the grand scheme of things, one can only pretend for so long in matters of the heart, so on what would have been their second wedding anniversary, she had to dissolve her marriage. This came as a blow to her parents because their religious convictions forbade divorce and remarriage. Beatrice never fails to inform Mel that Cahal had died from a broken heart, a heart that she, Mel, had stomped on in her desire not to be reconciled to her husband. Shortly after the divorce, Mel discovered that she was with child and knew that it was not Nolan's because loneliness had pushed her in the arms of Timothy one time too many. This was another blow to her parents and Mel just decided that she would just spend the rest of her life making amends to her parents.

Not long after, she gave birth to premature twin girls, Crystal and Topaz. They were very ill at birth and Beatrice never failed to inform poor Mel that the sins of the parents had been *visited on the children*. Of course, this inspired so much guilt in Mel that she would therefore do anything to appease her family. Through a lot of prayer and loving attention the girls flourished and are now exceptional second graders. Mel was ever so grateful for the support of her sister Val and her best friend, Cora, who spent so much time at the house that she eventually married Amethyst and had his three children, Amethyst Jr (AJ), Jasper and little Emerald who was born just a year ago.

To this day, no one knows if it is actually a love marriage or a marriage of opportunity or convenience. Mel dare not ask, because she has her own problems and although she had been friends with Cora for so long, she did not think it was her place. Plus, Cora came from the right social class, a socialite in her own right and is both beautiful and intelligent so in the end, everyone was happy. Invariably, it also helps that Cora loves to travel so most of their marriage was spent on separate continents. At first, Cahal and Beatrice were appalled but Amethyst assured them that all was well and it was best for their marriage that they spent some time apart. That was indeed a new concept to the Whiley's but Amethyst and Cora was always so enamoured around them that pretty soon their fears were allayed. Eventually, everyone got used to them spending time apart since they all recognised that it was ironically the great distance between them that kept their love alive and their marriage afloat. Never mind that Amethyst was missing important milestones in the lives of his children and their grandparents on both sides were missing out these turning points as well. Cahal tried unsuccessfully to explain that *it was not good for the man to be alone* to which Amethyst always responded that he was never alone, how could he be in such a huge family and he always added with a sly grin that 'absence made the heart grow fonder'. None of it made much sense to anyone but eventually they surmised that it was their life; hence, their choice.

Mel could not help but muse that she would never be allowed to do that, not in a million years. She grew to accept her life choices and willed herself to give up Timothy for the good of the cause. Timothy doesn't even know that he is a father. This saddens Mel immensely because in her heart she knows that he would be a phenomenal father but again, for the good of the cause, he had to remain in ignorance. She hated to think that all their lives her girls would come to believe that their dad had divorced their mum right when she was pregnant because the topic of their paternity was a well-kept secret in the Whiley family.

****

Amethyst

The twins were born when Cahal was way past his prime and it both humoured and flattered him to think that he had produced a son in his old age. Although not as old, he felt like God had shined down on him and had truly blessed his loin, just as he did for Abraham. Therefore, the twins became the apple of his eyes; especially, Amethyst who was blessed with all the strong features of the Whileys; eyes, complexion, temperament, right down to his very blonde hair.

The problem was and is still manifesting itself should be that Amethyst was Chahal's favourite child. He tried to hide it as much as he could but it was one of those not so well-kept secret in their family. Notwithstanding, as a child Amethyst was as demanding as he was impetuous which made him reckless. But as an adult he is both duplicitous and unscrupulous borne from an inbred sense of privilege. A privilege that came with lots of money; a deadly combination. Cahal always enjoyed a good chuckle when he overheard the child imposing his will on others. However, as Amethyst got older, it became increasingly obvious that qualities which had endeared him as a child made him both churlish and pernicious as an adult. Indeed, Amethyst is a master strategist which makes him invaluable to Whiley Inc. and Whiley Holdings.

Throughout his schooling, it was obvious that Amethyst was a leader and he was quite sure to make everyone aware of this fact. In high school he was team captain for almost every club imaginable but he really enjoyed the debate club, the most. It came as no surprise to anyone when Amethyst entered law school and was the top of his class from day one and valedictorian as well; decidedly, a high-achiever. That being so, it wasn't long before Amethyst started to feel a hankering for supremacy over the Whiley brood.

Now of course, Mason was the next in line for the throne; however, Cahal had unwittingly left an impression on Amethyst that he should have been in charge, that things might somehow run more smoothly. Therefore, Amethyst grew up believing that he was the rightful heir. Despite coming of age and obviously seeing how things were laid out in the family, Amethyst still believed that he should be in charge. Of course he never gave voice to this idea because clearly, he was way too smart for that but his subtle actions often proved that this was the case. For instance, he would go behind Mason and give different instructions to the staff which would lead to enough confusion to make Mason look inadequate. This is exactly how Amethyst preferred to operate; in that, he functioned in an in between place where he was as subtle as a serpent while being as direct as a spent arrow. Their staff often wondered if Mason was just too naïve because he never seemed to pay attention to the fact that his baby brother was undermining him. After a while, people just agreed that they were brothers and that it was none of their business.

Over the years Amethyst had become inordinately ambitious and this made him dangerous. He has always felt that since in his capacity as administrator of commerce, etc. he is literally the face of the business; hence, he should be in charge. The sad truth is that he really likes Mason, admires him *almost* but Mason is much too prudent. He is stuck in the old ways of doing things. He wasn't willing to take risks and establish contacts by any means necessary.

Therefore, Amethyst decided that he was going to show his big brother how to handle the business.

I had turned over the idea of a coup in my mind for a while, I decided to let it go because in order for that to work, my spineless siblings would have to be on board and they would never go against Mason. None of them would, not even my twin Mel. Let's face it, everyone likes the guy and respects him. Mason is one of those people in the world who naturally exudes so much confidence that he is given acclaim without even demanding or requiring it. He is so self-assured that those things mean nothing to him but I get this deep urge inside me that it is time for a shift. It is time to change how thing have always been done in this family. I keep telling myself that these things take time but I can't wait. I feel strongly that time is of the essence and I need to act now, to proverbially strike while the iron is hot.

After observing that malcontent Valin Finley watching our house for a while, I decided to forge ahead with my plan and to include him as well. Chloe's disappearance was the inciting incident I needed to activate my plan.

The mountains surrounding Emersyn, the mountain surrounding Emersyn has always been a sense of pride and protection for the family. But while it conjures all these positive emotions, we all know how dangerous it is to be in the mountains. There are all types of wild animals that we have spotted on the path to the mountain, the trees are so thick that cell phones don't work and can obscure one's vision. Forget about climbing the mountain at night or in the winter. While growing up, we have lost a number of pets to that mountain. Also, we once had a very audacious nanny who decided to hike up the mountain, somehow got lost and was found a week later. She actually was able to summit the mountain but getting there took her so long that she ran out of food and water before she got to the peak. Plus, while the air is really fresh and clean at the summit, it is also extremely cold; absolutely, no place for a lone human let alone a female.

****

137

Melisandre

Deep in my heart, I know better than to engage with Thyst and his plans. Every single time I let him talk me into one of his schemes, no good comes of it. So, when he told me to just take the short cut down from the mountain, the path away from the house and that he would meet me and explain later; I should have said a strong no. Apparently, we no longer needed to find Chloe because after a quick phone call to God knows who, he said it was Mason, but I don't think so there was something in his tone which just did not suggest that he had been talking to Mason, he would have had to be more respectful. Plus, there was just too much whispering.

Anyways, on my way down, when I was almost out of the mountain, I felt someone grab me from behind. I tried screaming but he had covered my mouth with a cloth that smelled so horrible that I am not even sure if I had passed out or if I had been drugged. Before I passed out, I remember thinking what will become of my girls? Who would raise them and who would love them if something bad happened to me? At that moment, I know I had to fight to stay alive for the good of my children because I have seen enough movies to know that nothing good ever comes of someone being kidnapped.

Here I am in the trunk of a musty car driving like one hundred miles per hour. I really hope that Amethyst comes to my rescue and worse that this was not a part of his plan. My mind is going as fast as this car and my breathing is laboured. I don't know how much more of this I can take. I can hardly breathe because of the cloth still in my mouth. I can't move because the space is too tight and worse I am severely claustrophobic. I can hear my heartbeat like a snare drum in my ears. I am sweating all over. My natural inclination is to kick, scream and fight to live but based on my current situation, this is counterproductive. I am actually doing more harm to myself than good but in my panic, there is not one logical thought left in my head. I am starting to feel lightheaded, this time I just give in to the darkness that overwhelms me. I actually wonder *is this is where my story ends?*

Is this where I die? Someone, anyone, please help me! My children, what will become of them?

Chapter Twenty
Loss

"All deaths are sudden, no matter how gradual the dying may be." – Michael McDowell

Everest

Everest is the youngest Whiley offspring and a wild child in every sense of the word. He came at a time when both Cahal and Beatrice were way past their springtime so he was allowed to roam free. In fact, he was primly reared by servants and his siblings. But from very early it was clear that he had a mind of his own and a temper to match. He excelled in sports and everything that was hands-on. He was definitely not meant for the boardroom and he was fine with that. He absolutely did not envy Mason's position in the family. He felt like that place in the family would have been too confining; hence, claustrophobic for him which would invariably lead to his death. Plus, he has an unbridled devotion to Mason.

Everest and Andira met straight out of college and fell passionately in love. This is sometimes confusing for bystanders when they fight but they are of the same temperament. Their passions are often at odds but ironically it links them inextricably to each other. Andira is an only child and is also accustomed to having her own way which is the primary source of fighting between them. They are each other's support system and are fiercely loyal to their individual families. Most people don't know that much of their fights is driven by the hedonism of unrestricted make up sex.

They both want children but on their own terms and in their own time, not just because it is the thing to do. They both share the same compassion for Mel, who they believe have been robbed of a life of her own. They have made secret vows to never allow that to creep into their union.

After walking around in the mountain for what seems like hours, with our feet aching and suffering from starvation; we return home. I couldn't wait to get away from Amelia and Andira, they both share the same propensity for complaining. I am still mad at Mason for putting them on the same search team with me. Eventually, we decide to return home and take the short cut (a path we had discovered when we were kids) as we figured one of the others must have found Chloe by now but our phones don't work at this altitude and the density of the trees also block the cell signals as well.

By now it is late afternoon and the afternoon sun is still a brilliant yellow that seems to wash over us after leaving the coolness of the mountain behind. On our way home, I start to feel an unease in the pit of my stomach. As soon as we step onto the back porch of Emersyn I discover why. There are police officers in our house and walking around in the backyard. They try to block us from entering the house, but I adamantly assure them that we live here so therefore they do not have the right to prevent us from entering our own home. As a result of the expanse of Emersyn, I obviously couldn't see the front of the house but I could safely assume that police officers were there as well. Did someone call the police because Chloe went missing? It must be Mason, he is the one who is always pandering to that cat, so much that she thinks she is human.

I walk into our living room and as soon as I saw the look of doom and gloom on all the faces, I knew immediately that something was terribly wrong and it wasn't Chloe this time. No one would be this upset about her; in all honesty, everyone would be glad to be rid of her. She was always getting into things, pooping everywhere except in her box, fighting with mum, crying loudly for no other reason; except that she thought that she was human. I remember one time, when Ms Chloe had gotten the bright idea in her feline head that she wanted to sleep with Mum. When Mason, finally, pulled her out of Mum's bed, kicking and screaming, she literally cried for the whole night. It is as if she decided that she couldn't sleep where she liked to as no one would get a lick of sleep.

The following night, she started with the tom foolery and it was one of the kids who made an astounding observation – although I'm not quite sure which one now – it might have been AJ because that kid is super smart, or MJ; anyways, whoever it was noticed that Chloe was afraid of the dark so she wanted to sleep with Mum because her light was always on even during the day. Mum decided a while back that being in the dark meant that your deeds were evil and seeing that she is such a God-fearing person, she couldn't afford to be found in the dark and

Daddy agreed, although he hated sleeping with the lights on. I couldn't help but think, *these are the people I come from. Shit!* Well, that night, Mason gave Chloe, a big fluffy bear to lay her dainty head on, a small bear to cuddle with and her very own *Elsa and Anna* night light. Heck, I wish they would let her go, where it is really, really cold as I am pretty sure the cold bothers her. She slept like a baby. From that night until now, Chloe always slept with her toys and night light because outside of that no one would be able to sleep. We discovered that, a few weeks later when the night light suddenly stopped working in the middle of the night, Ms Chloe woke up to darkness and cried so loudly and so much that she woke up everyone in the house. I really hate Chloe!

It was Amethyst's expression that summoned me out of my reverie. I have never seen that prick of a brother of mine looking like this before. He who is always acting high and mighty. The only person in this house he has fooled is Mason. We all see him for the subversive dissident that he is. Then I asked, 'What happened? Did you guys find Chloe?' I wish I hadn't asked. Val summed up the whole wretched business and said the inconceivable. She said it with a faraway look in her face, as if she were looking elsewhere, anywhere, just somewhere outside herself for the answer.

Val has always been soft spoken, but she said it so quietly, I had to ask her a few times to repeat it and that's when Gabe lost it and yelled, "MUM IS DEAD! CHLOE KILLED HER AND MEL IS MISSING!"

Amethyst suddenly made eye contact with me – because he too was looking off into space with his face turned towards the mountain as if all the answers to the world's problems reside there – and said, in a very demure voice, 'Happy now!' I said, 'Happy? Is this your version of a good news story of a happy ending?' I was about to punch out his lights, arrogant prick, but Emery intervened. He must really think that I am afraid of his bravado. While I was still trying to process all that Gabe and Val had said, I realised that Mason was missing. I was genuinely afraid to ask. Thankfully, Amelia beat me to it.

"So where is Mason?"

Emery, very quietly explained that, "Mason had to leave the hospital (nothing more could be done for Mum) and head straight to the police station because Chloe had brought home a human bone."

"So how do they know it's a human bone?" No one had a clear answer to this. Apparently, the shape and something else. Everyone was just dazed and confused like a football player who has been hit in the head with the ball. The bone had startled Mum and gave her a heart attack.

I almost laughed at the absurdity of the whole thing. I need a strong drink.

How could any of what they said be possible? But the police officers are there. Apparently, they are looking for the rest of the corpse. Suddenly, I wished that I hadn't come home, that I had stayed in the mountains looking for Chloe because if I were still in the mountain, I would not be hearing this so it would not be real.

****

Amoury

I examine all the sad weary faces in the room. I feel like an intruder. I don't know if I should sit, stand or leave the room. This is such a horrible thing to have happened to Mrs Whiley, although I never got the chance to meet her. She is obviously someone's mum and a huge part of their soul has been ripped out by this sudden tragedy. It is one thing to wait and watch someone who is ill die but it is quite another to see someone who otherwise is healthy die under such bizarre circumstances. Besides, where would Chloe find a human bone? Where might that have come from? Why has it suddenly appeared? So many questions! I really hope the police officers searching around outside will be able to shed some light on this matter in due season. I feel really horrible for this family; especially, Mason.

Of such, I really have to get to Mason and have a talk with him before anyone else does. There are far too many things happening at the same time, too many moving parts and I have a feeling that they are not just random but they are all connected. I finally realise who the 'insider' is who gave me access to Mason and I know for sure that Mel's disappearance is absolutely not a coincidence. Something is very wrong here and Mason potentially could be in a lot danger. There seems to be a miscalculation here and the 'insider' is probably nervous, which would make him extremely dangerous.

Amethyst

I have been calling that reject Valen all afternoon and it goes straight to voicemail. How difficult was it to just drug my sister to make her compliant and then take her to the destination that I had specified? Good help is so hard to find these days. I really hope that nincompoop has not harmed my sister, because if he has I am going to kill him with my bare hands. I knew I should not have trusted him with such a delicate procedure because he is a scoundrel but what else could I do? Time was running out.

I don't think Amoury knows that I am the one who he has been communicating with all these months. But he is a lot smarter than I thought he would be so it is only a matter of time before he starts making connections. That being said, at this point, I really don't care about anything else, I just really want my sister back. I want my life to go on as it was before. Mason can continue being head honcho, I am just desperate to have my sister back and I would do absolutely anything to make that happen. Unquestionably, nothing else matters as this point. Potentially, my actions have not been prudent over the last little while and this unequivocally may have cost the life of my sister, the only person (apart from my kids) that I care about in this whole wide world. A really high price to pay for my folly. To add to all that, Mum just died because of stupid Chloe, if I see her around here I am going to snuff out all her nine lives, all at once.

I really need to talk to Mason before anyone else. He will know what to do because at this point I can't think straight, all my thoughts, all my horrible thoughts have become one ugly mass of broken flesh that used to be my sister. That's all I can see every time I close my eyes. They say that twins are inextricably linked and of such can feel what each other is feeling; well, if that is the case, nothing good can or will come of what I am feeling. I feel like I'm about to lose my mind.

Chapter Twenty-One
A Quandry

*"Regeneration can come only through a change of heart in the individual." –
Henry Williamson*

Mason

It's been a full week now since my sister went missing and Mama died.
I can't find it in me to have a funeral for Mama while Mel is still missing so I've
been delaying the inevitable. It doesn't seem right. When we do have Mama's
home going service all of her kids should be present and accounted for. I simply
don't know what to do. The police have been following leads but so far nothing
concrete. It seems like there's a misfit, a Valin Finley who had been hanging
around, looking at Emersyn. But this means nothing as people come from miles
around to gaze at her grandeur so he probably was just in awe and kept returning.
I am not going to assume anything at this point. I need clear cut facts in order to
be able to make an appropriate decision. In a sad, horrible way, it is probably a
blessing in disguise that Mama passed when she did because Mel being missing
would have been too much for her to bear.

Moreover, everyone wants to talk to me these days, the police, Amoury,
Everest even Amethyst. I wonder what he has to say to me that is suddenly so
urgent. Meanwhile, I don't have the heart to speak to him right now. He must be
going through hell. I know that Amethyst can be difficult but I believe deep down
he really has a good heart, he is in some ways just like a child. He has an idealist
notion of how the world should work. He hasn't yet quite accepted that the world
works the way it will and there is nothing that us humans can or will do to prevent
the world from turning as it should. Speaking about child, I don't even know
what to tell Mel's twins, each time they look at me with those beautiful, brown
sad eyes, I die a little inside. How can I explain to seven-year-olds that in addition
to their grandma being dead, their mum might also be dead? Because as much as

I don't want to think about it, that is also a distinct possibility and the police have made it plain that the longer we take to find her, the greater the chances that she might already be dead. Oh, sweet Jesus! Please, God, let it not be so.

On top of all that, there is this whole matter of a body being buried somewhere in mountain. According to the Special Victim's Unit, although they have not found the rest of the corpse as of yet, based on the advanced state of decomposition of the bone that Chloe brought back, the body has been there for a while but the torrential down pour over night must have uprooted it. Plus, some animal might have been digging at the spot before the rains came. Nothing over the last little while makes any good sense. Then there is also DNA evidence which indicates that the deceased is a close relative. They have me going through the family archives to discover if any of my family members had gone missing. Oh, dear God! I hope this is not a case of history repeating itself.

I have been putting off talking to the guys this whole week but I can't do that any longer. Indeed, I need to take a break from going through this list of people long dead. I'm going to have to speak with them eventually and since Amoury is my guest, I guess I will start with him. Hopefully, there will be no more bad news for this week. I just cannot deal with any more negativity. My head is about to explode.

I so wish that Daddy were still here. This would have been his mess to sort out.

****

Amoury

Mason has finally made the time to see me. This whole week has been complete torture. I am constantly looking over my shoulder to check if I am safe. The only time I feel any type of peace is when I look out at that mountain near the house. Surprisingly, it brings a calmness to my mind that is completely out of context right now. Anyways, I am just going to go in there and just spill my guts. I could care less what happens after that. I knock a few times on his office door and he meets me at the door. He looks tired and worn out but that edge of confidence is still evident. Some people are just born leaders. After everything, this guy has still managed to maintain his composure all through this way from hell.

145

"Hey, Mason, I know you are really busy right now, but there is something urgent that I really have to say to you."

"Hey, come on in, Amoury! So very sorry that I have been such a poor host…"

"Don't worry about me! I know you have a whole lot on your mind."

"Please, come in and make yourself comfortable."

"Thank you."

I walk into his austere but stylish office; the room definitely reflects his self-assurance. He does not need a lot of elaborate furnishing to prove his worth. I used to be like that at one point in my life although I can't remember when. What has become of me? I feel like such a fraud. I feel like I am the one who is decorated, over dressed, wearing the integrity that belongs to someone else. This garment that is mine, yet not mine, hangs on me heavily. Its virtuous texture mocks me; I want to shake it off but yet I must wear it to perpetuate the show. When did I become a smear on humanity?

I sit on the edge of the comfortable leather chair and suddenly, I am overcome with such a deep sense of embarrassment, it renders me speechless. I can't face him! I can't tell him. It is way too humiliating. Yet I must! So much is riding on me right now. Mason looks at me in a peculiar way as if he is trying to discern my thoughts while at the same time, wanting to get this done and over with. He clears his throat.

"You wanted to speak with me, Amoury? I don't mean to rush you but I have a meeting with Amethyst right after so…"

At the sound of his sibling's name, I am jolted back into reality, my reality. A reality that is all consuming, but nevertheless, it is still mine. I say, a little too quiet,

"Yes, I do. But I have one request to make of you…"

"What's that, Amoury?"

"Please don't interrupt until I am finished. It is really, very difficult for me to say. Yet I know I must."

"Amoury, are you in some kind of trouble? You are beginning to scare me."

"Yes, I am! I am in deep dodo, in way over my head."

He immediately puts on his hat of authority and said with a sigh, "Let's hear it then."

He sounds so deflated. I am really sorry to be the bearer of such bad news.

Mason

Amoury comes to my office, looking weighed down like he is *Atlas*, carrying the whole world and its problems on his shoulder. For a man who has been overly anxious to speak with me all week he is mighty quiet. I suspect that something is not quite right with him, he has morphed into someone else, a stark contrast to the man I met only a week ago. For starters, his striking green eyes are now dull, he looks pale and somehow shorter and smaller, a mere shadow of himself. Also, he seems to be avoiding eye contact which is quite off-putting because one of his features that endeared him to me was his ability to look me in the eye. Over the years, dealing with so many people, I have discovered that the ones who are unable to look you dead in the eyes are particularly dangerous. I did not perceive that in him at all. Could I have been so wrong about him? Was Mum right all along? How could someone change so drastically in such a short time? Is it possible that I have misread him entirely? Oh, dear God, more bad news! I can feel it coming.

I clear my throat, as a not so subtle hint for him to get on with it. But the moment I mention Amethyst, his whole demeanour changes. Come to think of it, Amethyst has been acting weirdly as well and I get a sense that it is not just because Mel is missing. I have known Mr Amethyst all my life and I know for certain that he does not care about anyone but himself. He would sell Mum into slavery, if it meant that he could get a hold of the Whiley estate. I have known this for a while now and although Mauve has always insisted that I take drastic action against him, yet I chose not to because no matter what he *is* my little brother. Plus, let he that is without vice, cast the first stone. No one is void of vices so no one can. That being said, if I do discover that these two are in cahoots and have somehow caused the demise of my sister, there will be hell to pay. They will both wish that their green eyes never opened at the moment of their birth.

Chapter Twenty-Two
The Confession

"The confession of evil works is the first beginning of good works." – Augustine

Amoury

Mason is starting to look angry now and who can blame him.

"Amoury, quit stalling and get to the point. I don't have all day."

"OK, I will! I am sorry!"

This is what happened.

"I have been checking out your family for a while now…"

"Yes, you and a million others. Go on!"

"I know I am asking a whole lot of you but please don't interrupt. This is really hard for me to divulge but I will answer all your questions at the end."

"As you wish."

"Thank you. I honestly, don't know where to begin."

"Start from the beginning, Amoury, and tell me everything."

"So, like I said, I have been checking out your family online but not for the reason you think. You see, I am your cousin."

At this last comment, his brows furrow and the right one is slightly raised. But like a true gentleman, he keeps his word and says nothing.

My great, great, great, great, great, great, grandfather is Laika Cardinal and he was the son of Lance Jr Whiley. He was one of many mixed children born to slave women fathered by the Whiley men of that generation (hence my green eyes like yours). He was treated unfairly by his father and half siblings but to be honest, I don't really know all the details. He literally had to flee for his life, barely escaping at the last minute. He ran away to the north and did quite well for himself as he was a man of prudence and he could spot opportunities a mile away. He met and fell in love with my great, great, grandmother and became the custodian of the Cardinal heritage since they had no male heirs. Cardinal is actually his wife's maiden name. However, there was a wound in his soul, from being mistreated by the Whileys. Therefore, on his death bed, he left a declaration that has lived on through the generations, that none of us should rest until Emersyn falls. Over the years, many people have tried and failed but here I am in my turn to ensure that this happens. But since I met you I have been conflicted because I suspect that you are a decent person; hence, you should not be made to pay for the sins of your fathers. It would be akin to asking me to atone for Laika's sins.

****

Mason

At first, I can't believe what Amoury is saying. I actually start to look around for a camera, thinking any minute now, those guys from the Netflix show *Prank Encounters* are going to leap out at me. But based on the tortured look in his eyes, I know that this is no prank, neither is it a television show. What have I gotten myself into? He goes on to say.

After attempting to reach out to you for a while and failing, I decided that I was going to give up. But then I got a call from someone working with an insider at your company. This person, claimed to know about Laika and said that his family was wronged as well. Also, that he is in pursuit of justice for his family and finally he was now working with someone close to you who could help us exact revenge. At first, I hung up on him and told him never to contact me again. However, he just kept calling and eventually, I relented. I listened to his plan. I don't even know why I did because this is not me. I am an academic. I just felt a strong urge to meet you and I was angry that you refused at every turn, even refusing to take my call. Plus, I felt the weight of the expectations of my forefathers, people whom I have never met but feel a strong connection to them. Much like I feel connected to you, Mason.

Anyways, we came up with a plan based on an observation that I had made while I was in South Africa. The local farmers use a product called Ag-Lime – which is actually crushed lime stone – as a pesticide. But from my discussion with them, it is very important that the right quantity is applied or else it will

149

have an adverse effect on the produce. So, as you know, I am proposing a very new fertiliser that's not yet on the market – which in and of itself is an excellent product – I have personally tested it, doing the research and everything. However, the plan was, that I would add Ag-Lime to the fertiliser, far more than the required amount and the Ag-Lime would interact with the fertiliser and pretty soon, your beautiful apple orchards and your lush landscape would have been destroyed. Emersyn would lose her value and I could swoop in and purchase it for a penny on the dollar.

At that, he paused for a moment as if looking for congratulatory remarks. Notwithstanding, I am so absolutely stunned that I wouldn't even know exactly what to say. He gets up and spaces back and forth, then he seems to settle on an idea.

I am not sure, who the insider is; but even so, I strongly believe that the insider is your brother Amethyst and please don't ask how I know because I just do. Also, I am of the view that Melisandre's disappearance is directly linked to this nefarious plan of ours. I am starting to get scared because usually I would be in touch with my guy on the phone but somehow he has disappeared. I have not heard anything from him, not a word which is quite unusual. Still and all, what is even more perplexing is that the last time we spoke (the first night when I arrived here) he said he was afraid of the insider. He sounded really scared. Like I said, I don't know for sure how Amethyst is involved but my gut tells me that he is and not only that but based on Melisandre's disappearance, he is being reckless and impulsive which means, he is running scared so he is particularly dangerous. Therefore, that is why I feel compelled to share this with you because I don't believe you are not safe either. Every time, I think of this, our sordid affair, I have a really horrible feeling in the pit of my stomach.

Now, he realises that this is wrong and that he has made several mistakes! Now, he has a bad feeling about this. Now, that he feels exposed, he is running to me to rescue him. I should shoot him right here and now. But I feel like I need him to smoke out Amethyst. Because as angry as I am at Amoury, for some reason I believe the piece about Amethyst and I am furious at him for bringing so much danger to our doorstep and for possibly causing the death of his twin sister. One thing about Amethyst, unlike Amoury, he will never confess his sins.

His hubris won't let him. That traitor! I should just shoot both him and Amoury. But if I shoot them both, I might never know what happened to poor Mel, like a lamb to the slaughter, she was dragged into Amethyst's schemes and plans because of his selfish ambition which has blinded him to being prudent. I bet he never thought this would or could happen.

Without giving any of my thoughts away, and with a calmness that I don't even possess, I give Amoury, the snake, very clear and specific instructions that he needs to leave my office immediately and not to do anything without consulting me first. Also, if he hears from his weaselly friend then he should contact me right away. I instruct him to stay in his room and keep the door locked.

In the meantime, I have to meet with Amethyst. I know there is something up with him and it is not just about Mel's disappearing.

✱✱✱✱✱✱✱✱✱✱✱✱

Amethyst

All of a sudden, everywhere is pitch black. I try to cry out but no one can hear me. I am suffocating, almost as if I am drowning despite the fact that there is no water. I look around and I see Mason. He is standing on top of the mountain near Emersyn, he is looking down as if, in search of something; I try screaming for Mason to come get me but my voice won't come out. My voice is paralysed, which is strange because I can run and move, all my extremities work, just not my voice. I feel like I have been muted. Is this how it feels being voiceless? Is this how it feels to be calling for help and everyone is around yet no one hears your voice?

I am starting to panic, although, I have never in my life experienced a panic attack I feel like one is coming on. I tell myself, *just breathe! Everything is fine! Just breathe!* Although even as I am saying this to myself, I know intuitively that nothing will ever be the same ever again. In my mind's eye, I see myself, I look savage and uncultured. Is this what is left of me? Is this what I am going to be moving forward?

As I slowly come out of my dream – thankfully, it is just a dream – I hear really loud screaming and I wonder what is wrong? Who could be screaming like that? Only to discover that is me. My throat aches from all the screaming, my sheets are soaking wet, drenched in sweat and tears. This is about the third time this week that I am having this dream and it is really weird for me because I am one of those people who almost never dream. Plus, when I do dream, it is never this horrifying. Is this how Mel is feeling right now? Oh, dear God, we have to find her.

I look at the time and it is after nine in the morning. I am never in bed this late on a week day but I have been fighting all these nightmares and horrible thoughts that it keeps me up at nights. My head feels cloudy, like when I was a child and I had the flu accompanied by a high temperature, that terrible feeling at the high point at the peak of the fever. A new detail has manifested today, I keep hearing voices; however, none that I am able to recognise. I just hope I can hold it together when I meet up with Mason. The last thing I want is for Mason of all persons to think that I am crazy.

I get out of bed with a new resolve. I have to tell Mason, what is really going on, even if he is going to hate me forever and throw me out of Emersyn. I cannot go on like this any longer. Normally, when I have a secret this huge, I have Mel to share it with but now that she's not here, I have no one to share it with and it is quite rigorously eating away at me. It is frantically eating away at my *ego*, soon only the *Id* will remain. There's no telling what kind of mess that will initiate. Wasn't it Freud who said, '*The ego represents what we call reason and sanity, in contrast to the id which contains the passions.*' Or was that Erickson? Who knows? I don't know much anymore, except that I might have lost my sister and best friend out of a desire to possess what was never meant to be mine. Isn't that the rudiments of the human condition? I have lost so much pursuing what was never mine, neglecting what was truly mine. I have not seen my wife and kids in over three months. I wonder if my kids got taller or plumper.

I take a quick shower to wash of the dregs of the nightmare, I must not carry it with me into my day. What I am about to do, will take all the strength I have left which is miniscule. I feel like David on his way to confront Goliath.

It's time to end this.

＊＊＊＊＊＊＊＊＊＊＊＊

Mason

As soon as I am done with Amoury, I get a text from Amethyst that he needs to see me and that I need to meet him by our Poplar tree aka Buddy. I wonder aloud, why would he want me to meet him there? This could easily be a trap, a part of his plan to get rid of me, I better bring my gun for protection. Because if he is packing so am I.

I tell Mauve that if I am not back in the house after thirty minutes, she should call the cops. She looks really frightened like a child. Marigold looks so much like her, with her ultra-black hair and dazzling hazel eyes. As I kiss her good bye, I muse on what a lucky man I am.

I can't help but think of Amethyst's preposterous marriage, with his wife and kids gone half the time. What kind of life is that? There were so many other beautiful, intelligent, eligible young women who Amethyst could have married but instead he chose Cora. God alone knows why. She was always way too impulsive and that is a huge part of the problem with their marriage. As soon as she gets a hitch to go to some *exotic location* (her words not mine), she just ups and leaves with the kids. No wonder Amethyst is so unhappy and has so much time on his hands to plan these ridiculous schemes; instead of, playing catch with his kids, teaching them to read, teaching them the way of the Whileys, embedding in them a sense of pride in their heritage. Needless to say, how could he, when they are always half the world away. Plus, who knows if Cora is being faithful. Anyways, that's none of my business. I have always felt that situation was not ideal but as usual Amethyst would not listen. He had to do things his way.

I step out into the early morning sun and let its rays wash over me as if to cleanse me from all my anxiety and the insanity that is gradually unfolding around me. The morning is fairly cool, not yet overpowered by the heat of the sun. It is such an ordinary day, all the birds singing their favourite song, the wind is making the trees dance in harmony, the flowers are looking so happy to see a new day, with their faces turned up, towards the sun; even Chloe was in a good mood this morning. Chloe is so completely oblivious to all the mayhem she has caused. I have to watch her with Everest because he has never liked her and now he is threatening to kill her. This thought brings back sobriety in my world because the way things are now, absolutely nothing is normal, nothing is as it should be. A quick review of the facts only legitimises this idea.

1. Chloe disappeared and while we were out looking for her, she got home before us.
2. Mum is dead because Chloe found a human bone and brought it into the house.

3. We searched for Chloe in teams, the twins were together but Amethyst returned without Mel.
4. Mel has been missing for a week.
5. My house guest and almost business partner has just confessed that he is my cousin and he has been scheming with an 'insider', someone apparently who is close to me, to destroy my life, to destroy everything that successive Whileys have attained because of a long-held vendetta.
6. Amethyst wants to see me in a very obscure location.
7. I don't trust my baby brother so I am carrying a gun and I intend to shoot first and ask questions later.

Absolutely nothing is the same and things will never be the same after today.

****

Amoury

Since my talk with Mason this morning, I do feel a little bit better, a little lighter. I have passed on some of my load to Mason. As per his instructions, I have been self-isolating in my exquisite room. I keep replaying the conversation in my head. I actually thought that Mason would have killed me with his bare hands but I guess true to his nature, he is still processing our conversation. I am not too sure what type of response I was expecting though. I basically told him that I have been plotting his demise almost my entire life.

I gaze through the window, for some reason, I keep going to the window to look at the mountain because looking at that mountain is so soothing for me and right now my jarred nerves are on edge and in desperate need of a calming elixir. Come to think of it, last week, I didn't get a chance to finish my hike, I should just go for a quick walk to clear my head. From what Mason says, police officers are supposed to be back today, to continue the search for the rest of the corpse that Chloe found. To think that, Chloe is responsible for so much mess in this house and she struts around without a care in the world. If it weren't so painful, it would be hilariously funny. From the looks she's been getting, I am pretty certain more than half the Whileys would like to bury her with the corpse that she found.

I can't just sit in this house; I am about to go stir crazy. I really want to go for a walk but I wouldn't want to get lost like Melisandre. Nevertheless, since the moment I got here, I feel like that mountain is beckoning to me, calling my name to venture into the unknown. The call is too great, too urgent; despite what Mason said about staying put, I have to go. I'll just bring my whistle so that if I get lost I can use it and hopefully someone will find me.

Mason

I approach our beautiful and ancient poplar tree, not knowing what to expect. As I step into its cool and familiar embrace, I remember a different time. A time when all my siblings and I would play right on this spot of ground protected by the lush branches of this tree. In the summer time we would play way into the evenings until the lights came on or mum came to get us. I remember, Amethyst really enjoying just being here with the rest of us, running around playing; Mel as well. But clearly that was a different time, now Mel has vanished without a trace and I am thinking horrible thoughts about ending the life of one of my baby brothers.

I hear a sound and I turn to see Amethyst coming through the opening where the branches make an arch. We lock eyes and his look is wild, weary and lost, like a sheep that drifted too far away from the flock and the shepherd. As angry as I am with him, the look on his face, his beautiful face has transformed, he now has bags under his eyes and his once glowing complexion has now gone pale. Normally, he carries pride and ego on his shoulders; hence, his shoulders are always erect but not today; his shoulders are like sturdy trees which have been battered by strong winds so they have slumped over. He is just a mere fragment of his former glory; his feet look like they weigh a ton. Seeing him like this, discovering his humanity, I just want to embrace him and tell him that everything was going to be OK. But my own sense of pride and honour won't let me. I have convinced myself that he has done the unforgivable; hence, unworthy of being forgiven; his evil deeds never to be forgotten; even before I heard his side of the story. But don't we all suffer from the human condition and in many areas of our lives, we need to be forgiven? Isn't that a requirement to being forgiven as well, to forgive others? *Forgive us our debt as we forgive our debtors.* Isn't this what is required of all humans?

A part of me really wants to console him; but on the other hand, I do not wish to lie to him either because to be honest, I do not yet have a clear sense of what is really happening here, neither do I know how to proceed. This is all new ground for me and the situation is still fluid; constantly evolving. Therefore, I do not wish to deceive him either and add to the long list of duplicitous acts which have been crafted against me. Yes, all these devices have been created to initiate my ultimate demise and terminate my legacy, to take away from my legacy and my son's inheritance. So, I do take all of this personally. Amoury, and I do also suspect that Amethyst as well, have fashioned a weapon which has the ability to result in my reign as head of the Whileys being marred by the destruction of everything us as people hold dear. So of course, this is going to be quite difficult for me to forget; forgo, forgive.

Amethyst walks to where I'm standing, to be clear, it's more like he staggers over to my general direction. Up close, all his new and sudden imperfections are magnified. I want to look away but I can't, I won't; he's proven that he cannot be trusted. I will never turn a blind eye to his machinations ever again. He is having trouble matching my gaze. Just like with Amoury, I clear my throat, an indication for him to get on with it. He opens his mouth but nothing comes out; again, just like Amoury. Apparently, the only distinguishing feature about them is their skin colour. They are the same type of snake. They are more like brothers than cousins. Eventually I declare,

"Is there something you have to say, little bro? I am quite sure that you didn't drag me out here for the ambience or to reminisce."

He starts, but has to clear his throat a few times to catch his bearings.

"I… actually, I did! I wanted you out here, in a spot that we used to play together so that despite what I am about to say, you will remember that I am still your little brother."

"Yea! Yea! Get on with it!"

My patience is wearing thin as it is. I am sick of the B.S. because clearly, he has invited me here to manipulate me again using nostalgia as a cover, my bond with him as a weapon. Who weaponised affection?

He continues, "I have a lot to share with you; therefore, I am going to request that you hold your questions until after."

At this, I can't help it. I laugh out loud, a bitter laugh almost like a bark, much like an injured coyote. He must really think this is one of his television appearances. I think he intended to say, applause – hold your applause. He is so accustomed to the acclaim; so much so, that it went straight to his head. Nevertheless, he begins,

I don't even know where to start but I am going to try to start from the beginning. But from the get go, I want you to know that I am really, really sorry. I did not mean for anyone to get hurt; least of all my twin sister.

I continue to stare him down. I can hardly stand to look at him but I must. Suddenly, all his imperfections vanish and he is the same arrogant knave that he has always been.

"Initially, all I wanted to do was prove my worth, to show you that I am fully capable of being a leader."

At this, I have to interrupt.

"Excuse me! But when was your ability to lead ever called into question? I don't ever recall a time or a place where that ever happened? If anything, Dad was always pandering to your every whim and fancy. So, excuse me, if I don't accept your B to the S. Maybe on a different day but most certainly not today."

I shriek, "Now quit stalling and get to the point. I don't have all day."

I really didn't mean to shout but I don't know who the hell he thinks he is trying to fool! Not me and certainly, not today.

He continues.

Anyways, whether or not you believe me, I have always admired you, your sense of calm in stressful situations, your work ethic and your self-confidence. You just have to walk into a room and you command respect. I truly wanted that. I just didn't want to be your little brother anymore walking in your shadow. I wanted to be seen, heard and respected just like you. When I came up with this plan, it was just so that I could prove my worth by showing initiative. So, this was the plan I devised. I admit now that it wasn't one of my brightest moments. But I assure you that my intentions were honourable. In my capacity as head of media and my connections to the black market, I heard that there was a product, an Ag-Lime. Apparently, this product is used as a pesticide in some parts of the world to kill weeds and some bugs, in small amounts but when used in a great quantity, it can lead to crop failure. Also, there is also an antidote, if you will, which is where Amoury comes in. He thinks that he would only be supplying the fertiliser but through my middle man, a Valin Finley, he would actually be supplying both and would be my fall guy for this whole operation.

He didn't actually know that I was the insider but as soon as I saw him, I knew that he would be my ticket to love and respect. Ultimately, after you went into business with him, to acquire this new ground-breaking fertiliser, he would supply you with a mixture of the Ag-Lime and fertiliser but later he would provide me with the right type and quantity of fertiliser to correct the damage to the orchards and then for once in my god damn life, I would be the hero and not you. For once, I would be worthy of respect from our siblings and staff because I know they talk about me behind my back. I know they say that I want to be you. I know they say I want to take your place. Some of them even want to take my place. I just know it. They are all conspiring against me and are all out to get me.

As head of this family, I see it as a part of my responsibility to ensure that everyone in this family is doing well; even Chloe sometimes to my chagrin. However, while Amethyst was declaring that *they* were all *conspiring against* him, almost foaming at the mouth, spit flying everywhere; all I saw was his decline into insanity – a beautiful, broken boy. He is shaking with consternation. He is even looking around him, wildly because I assume that he is of the view that *they* are watching him and *out to get him* any minute now. How did I not catch this sooner? Why was I not paying attention to my little brother's mental health? Amethyst is as mad as the *Hatter of Alice in Wonderland.* I have watched that movie enough times with my kids to know this. Apparently, all those lonely nights spent working late and having too much time on his hands have driven him to madness. He did not have a partner who valued him so he needed an outlet.

For a minute, I am forced to forget his deception and focus on his motives and state of mind, this is exactly what insanity looks like; textbook. I know this because, while I was searching through the annals of the Whiley clan, I discovered that we had a great, great, great, great Uncle Lawrence, who fought in the Civil War and returned broken. He started acting in the same way that Amethyst just exhibited and one day he just got up and left. It was believed that he had been '*harmed*' by an '*envious son of bitch*' (their words not mine) but there had been no proof of that. So, even in the sheriff's records, he is listed as '*missing and unaccounted for*'.

Caramba! I wish I could go back to hating Amethyst for his deception. Now all I feel for him is pity. He is rambling again!

"I see that you are planning to call the sheriff, aren't you? You are just trying to find a way to turn me in, aren't you?"

"You are against me as well!"

"No, Amethyst! Absolutely not! What are you saying?"

"I know you blame me for Mel's disappearance. Well, you know what? I blame me too. It was not supposed to end this way!"

"End what way? What are you talking about?"

"He was only supposed to kidnap her and keep her in a safe place so that while you are distracted I would convince you to leave me in charge and I would push through the deal with Amoury. None of this was supposed to happen."

"Slow down, little bro! None of what? What are you talking about?"

"But that darn Chloe! She went missing, then Mum died and I activated my plan too quickly!"

He is weeping now, wallowing on the ground. All his arrogance, gone with the wind. I am speechless at both his actions and his words. Between sobs, he states,

"I've been calling Valin this whole week and nothing... I haven't heard anything from him... now I don't know what to do... usually, he would pick up on the first ring but now he's not answering... I know that he is a low-life junky so I shouldn't have placed my sister's life in his hands. I am so, so, so sorry."

At that last comment, I am running towards the house because I have to call the sheriff and tell him this new piece of information which might save my sister's life.

I hear Amethyst say, "I should have been more prudent like you!"

As I am sailing towards the house, I pray quietly, *God please spare my sister's life. Let us get to her in time.* I hope we are not too late.

Chapter Twenty-Three
The Search

"Maybe you are searching among the branches for what only appears in the roots." – Rumi

Mason

I rush back to the house to find Amoury while I am dialling the police. Quite possibly Amoury might have access to more information even if he doesn't know that he has that info. I take the stairs two at time to get to his room but when I get there, he is gone. He is not in his room after I gave him clear and specific instructions to stay there. While am on the phone with the police, I search all the common areas. He is nowhere to be found.

I request to speak with Detective Lamont Friar but they put me on hold. After a brief wait, a very tired sounding Detective Friar comes on the line. His breathing is laboured as if he had to run to get the phone. He sounds just like I have been feeling lately. I feel as if I am losing my breath, my balance. I can't help but wonder, *Why did all this this have to happen on my watch? Why didn't this happen before Dad died? But then Amoury wouldn't be here if Dad was still around. Oh well!*

"Hello, this is Detective Friar. How may I help you?"

"Hey, this is Mason Whiley. You are currently investigating the disappearance of my sister Melisandre Whiley…"

He interrupts, "Hi, well we don't have anything new to tell you…"

"Listen, I think I have discovered some new evidence in this case. Can you please come out to Emersyn? It's urgent so please hurry."

"OK, sir! Me and my partner can be out there within the hour."

"OK, just hurry!"

I hang up feeling the feral hands of panic trying to grip my throat. I resist vehemently because I do not have any time to play her games, there's just too much at stake so I have to keep a clear head. I call Mauve on her cell, she is in the back garden with the kids.

"Have you seen Amoury today?"

"Yes, earlier I saw him heading towards the mountain."

It is a mystery to me why he would be heading towards the mountain, knowing fully well what happened to Mel. Forget that I told him not to leave his room. We'll just have to find him later. I really hope he doesn't get lost and I hope this is not part and parcel of another one of his deceptive plans. I tell her to meet me in my office ASAP. She's asking, 'Is there news?' When I hang up. I can't explain now. Next, I call Val, I give her the same directive. She too is wondering if there is any news.

I return to my office to wait for the girls. I look through my window and I see that the members of the special victim's unit are already gathered outside, some of them heading towards the mountain. The mountain looks so peaceful, giving up none of her secrets as to what might have happened there decades ago. I search the greenery to see if there might be a clue but as expected, there is none. The trees all seem to be in collusion trying their best to keep this secret. Hopefully, their search will be productive and we will soon discover who is buried in the mountain. They might even find Amoury in the mountains as well because I don't have a clue where he could be. I keep searching myself, wondering where I went wrong with Amethyst and how I could have been so deceived by Amoury. How could all this have happened right under my nose? Here I am thinking that I was being prudent. But ta da! Here we are!

In fifteen minutes, the three of us have convened in my office. I waste no time on preliminaries, I dive right into the account of the events as they were handed to me by both Amoury and Amethyst. I leave nothing out because of all the people living in this house I feel like these two are my support system and the only people I can trust. The girls are shocked but I don't have time to pacify them right now. I need their help in determining how much of what Amethyst told me is important to divulge to the police. Plus, of necessity I have to Dr Amoury's part as well, since he has the ability and the intelligence to sink Amethyst. After all, Amethyst is a Whiley and an unwell one at that; moreover, if what Amoury said is true, then he too is a Whiley but I have no time to figure that part out yet, that will have to wait until after Mel is home safe.

Also, now that we know that Mel had been captured, on the grounds of Emersyn, someone might have noticed something peculiar that day. In cases like these, even the most minute detail might be significant. Plus, I still need help in going through the archives to see what became of our great, great, great Uncle Lawrence. Although the police have not yet located the rest of the corpse, it would be good to be able to link it to an actual person. This is Whiley property so that must be a Whiley buried there; but which one? How did he or she come to be buried there without any formal rites?

The girls and I wrack our brains coming up with a plan; eventually, we do come up with a plan (not a great one since time won't allow for that) and not a moment too soon because true to his word Detective Friar is here within the hour. I just hope Amethyst stays out the way while he and his team are here. There is absolutely no point getting him involved in the state that he is in. Invariably, he will be detriment to himself.

****

Amoury

Mountains have always meant a lot to me. But these mountains are of special significance. Because the way I see it, Laika must have traversed these mountains at some point in time. My feet are actually touching the same grounds that my ancestors walked on and not just Laika but his family and the Whileys as well. Laika and his family members were all born into slavery. I can't help but wonder, if I am so drawn to South Africa because that's where my ancestors originally came from. That's one of the many atrocities of slavery, it robbed people like me the right to know where my origin began. I am quite sure it wasn't just here in Shrove.

I reasoned that, I had to get one last look at these mountains before I go to prison. I can't help but wonder if my ancestors would have been disappointed in me. Well, maybe not Laika, he would have been pleased. I most certainly am quite disappointed in myself. How could I allow myself to be corrupted like this? Formerly, I was a very intelligent person but I don't even know what has happened to me. I am pretty sure that Mason is going to call the police and tell them everything. I am for sure, for sure knee high in a lot of faecal matter right now and rightly so.

The day is so beautiful despite my quandary. It is weird that absolutely nothing is normal but the day is breathtakingly beautiful and routine. The birds are chirping like they normally would, the trees are dancing to the drumming of

162

the wind, the sky is a pale blue colour and not a cloud is to be seen anywhere. I don't see them yet, but I hear the little animals who call the mountain home, scampering around – just like any other day. Except this is not any other day, this is the day when I of necessity acknowledge what a low down, dirty scoundrel, weasel I am. And what's worse, I had to share this revelation with Mason. How will I ever face him again? How will I ever face Val again? Two of the most noble people I have ever met. My life is literally over. All my studies were in vain because here I am looking at a life sentence. A sentence which I have given myself.

These are my dark thoughts when I trip over something. I fall hard and heavy. I reach for my cell phone and turn on the torch to examine my surroundings. I immediately go into self-preservation mode trying to protect myself from any dangerous animals lurking in the vicinity. Imagine that! Meanwhile, I am the dangerous animal. Anyways, I look around and I come face to face with two eyes, staring unblinkingly back at me. I simultaneously scream and scramble to my feet. It is a body and the smell tells me it has not been long dead. What have I stumbled into?

I race down the mountain much like Mason did a week ago. Now I am the one who is running like a champion athlete. How could this day suddenly become creepier? Who the heck is that back there?

I race back to Emersyn and as soon as I disembark from the mountain, I see police cars. I think that they have come to get me. In the middle of my run, I am suddenly hit by the thought, what if they think I murdered this guy? I am already in enough mess as it is. Maybe I should just keep my mouth shut. I've confessed enough for one day. Doesn't that count for something? At this thought, I am disgusted with myself. Who knows if this is the universe's way of helping me to make amends? To somehow atone and cleanse myself of all the bad karma that I have been accumulating over the last little while. But it would be so easy to just return to my luxurious room and pretend that I did not just see too eyes glaring at me. Never mind, that I might never be able to sleep again since that would require me to close my eyes and there is no way I can do that without seeing those two eyes. I think, *Amoury why are you like this*? When did I become devoid of a backbone? It must be all the milk I have been drinking. I pledge right then and there to never drink milk again. Why do humans drink milk anyways? We don't need milk once we are grown? How am I still breathing God's good, clean air with everyone else when I have clearly become an abrasion on humanity?

I decide that I have to do what's right in this situation. I have to make my discovery known no matter what it will cost me. It might somehow be useful in tracking down Melisandre's abductors and absolve me of my unwitting participation in her situation. I gather speed again and I run straight into the arms of a very chubby police officer.

He grabs me and says, "Hey! Hey! Look where you're going, young man! What in the world is wrong with you?"

I think *too much*! I don't have time so I just say what I ran all the way here to say before I change my mind again.

I blurt out, "I saw a body in the mountain and he was staring at me!"

All of a sudden, I am light headed and nauseous. It must be the shock kicking in. And then, I do something that in all my life, I have never done. I faint.

****

Mason

All this moron had to do was stay in his room. He had one job, stay in his room. And here he comes running down the mountain like he just escaped out of hell declaring that he has just found a body. That's just wonderful! Chloe found a bone and he found a body. Jesus Christ what next?

He is lucky he fainted because I am so angry that I could literally shoot him, right here and now, in front of the police. Anyways, all the police who came to search for Chloe's body, now turn their attention to finding the new body.

On top of all that commotion, Amethyst emerges from the comforting fortress that is Buddy, saying that bees are attacking him! Meanwhile, there was not one bee to be found anywhere. Everyone tried to calm him down by reassuring him that there were no bees! But he was way too agitated. Finally, the police officers had to put cuffs on him for his protection and everyone else's. Imagine that, a Whiley in handcuffs, right here on the grounds of Emersyn! Good God, more insanity!

The police officers search all afternoon into evening, Amoury is still out like a light so they have to just trace his steps to the body. Word came late in the evening that they found the fresh body and the old one. They are calling the old body John Doe and the new one, they claim to know. Apparently, he is Amoury and Amethyst's accomplice. The question now is, if he is here and dead, then where in the world is Mel and is she dead as well?

Chapter Twenty-Four
The Aftermath

"New beginnings are sometimes disguised as painful endings."

Amoury

I woke up in the hospital with a severe headache. At first, I didn't even know where I was or what had happened. But as soon as I woke up and saw Val, sweet Val, all the horrible things I had done came rushing back to me. I wish I had stayed asleep. At first the tension in the room is palpable but eventually it simmers to a mere throb.

Val is not as angry as I thought she would be. I am unworthy of her compassion. She wanted to know how I was feeling and if I could sit up. Apparently, it was the shock that knocked me out. Thank God for shock. There are some very awkward moments when she is just staring at me. Meanwhile, I am staring at the wall. Invariably, she breaks the silence.

"Is what Mason said true? Are you really our cousin?"

"Yes!"

"Why didn't you say that from the get go, from the first night you came?"

At that question and comment, I had to snicker.

"So you would have me believe that you and your white, privileged would just accept a black man fresh off the street, claiming to be your cousin? Don't make me laugh, my head hurts."

"Really! After, all that you and Amethyst have done, you dare to judge us?"

Val raises her voice just a tad above her normal range.

"You know what is true, sir, on the night you came, not even, from in the day, me and a few of my brothers met up and all we talked about was how familiar you felt. Gabe really doesn't care about anything that goes on in this family. He has his own issues but he spoke up that night and said, there is something about you that resembles 'home', his words not mine."

"So, you would have me to believe that, you and your 'brothers' are so *woke* that you would just accept me like that? Again, don't make me laugh, it still hurts."

"No, I am serious, Amoury, we are not as horrible as you might think. If we were that horrible, the police would be here right now instead of me. I assure you, we do not want to get you in any unnecessary trouble..."

"You actually mean, that you do not want to let Amethyst in any trouble. Because, if I go down, he goes down."

"You have the nerve to sit in that bed and threaten my family? After all we've done for you?" Now she is really riled up and shouting.

"You could have been rotting in a cell somewhere; except, that we chose to protect you. Yes, in covering for you, we are covering for Amethyst, but guess what, right now he is so broken that no judge would convict him. So yes, we are protecting him and you as well because that's what us Whileys do, we look out for each other."

That really angers me.

"Oh, really now! Just like how your forefathers looked out for Laika, right? You people..."

"You people! Who the hell are you calling 'you people'. I am afraid that you very much have us confused with someone else. And you're right! If what you say about Laika is true..."

"IF! WHY WOULD I LIE?"

We are both going head to head when Mason bursts in.

"What is going on here? Amoury you should be resting! But I heard both of you from all the way down the hall. We are Whileys, so please act like it. Whatever the issue is, we will discuss in the confines of Emersyn, not here in this very public place. Do I make myself clear to you both?"

Val and I have been duly chastised and we look equally embarrassed. But as for me, I am so deeply touched that Mason and before that Val proclaimed me as a Whiley. They might be tricking me to protect Amethyst but even so – the very thought that despite all I have done, or planned to do – they would still consider me is very heart-warming. Now my embarrassment is complete. Suddenly, I know deep down, in the inner recesses of my soul, that this is all Laika ever wanted; to be included. To not be treated as *other* which he had been

166

all his life. This is what scarred his very soul and made him embittered so much so that no matter how much he had accomplished in his life time, it was never enough because the people he really wanted to impress and wanted to embrace him, see him as an equal, had rejected him publicly; time after, after time. Val interrupts my thoughts.

"See, Amoury, we do accept you as a Whiley. Regardless of what has happened, you are one of us and I think that is why you are the way you are."

We all laugh at this. Meaning, fully understood.

She continues, "It is not your fault nor Amethyst's. It is or it has become a genetic disorder for the Whileys to be, well topsy-turvy (for lack of a better word)."

Mason interjects.

"We have been going through old records and we have come to realise that the Whiley men especially have been less than gracious. But please understand, that we are not them. We are not like them. In fact, for many generations, both you and Amethyst are the first Whileys to act up this way."

Val's turn to chime in.

"That being said, we cannot be held accountable for the actions of our ancestors. Yes, they have committed a lot of atrocities but we CANNOT be made to pay for their sins. That would be quite similar to asking you to atone for the sins of Laika and your other ancestors in Africa who sold their brothers into slavery."

I am very upset again.

"Hold on a cotton-picking minute. You in your life of white privilege, dare to bring up what happened in Africa, many centuries ago, here and now, to justify hundreds of years of oppression from the white man. First of all, the slavery that existed in Africa was quite mild compared to what came to exist in the new world. I have been to Africa and that's the first thing I checked. Plus, when have you ever been blocked from any place because of your skin tone…"

I feel my blood pressure rising and my face getting red.

Mason touches my shoulder gently and says, "Easy there, big fella. Val is not justifying anything that our ancestors have done. She is merely trying to make a point about responsibility and accountability. And while that is important to the progression of humanity as a specie; however, being made to feel a sense of comradery in other people's misdeeds is grossly unfair. Plus, I've never understood that notion of white privilege, could you please explain it to me one day but not here, not now, not in this place."

"Yes, Mason, that's true, but that was cruel! I am sorry, Amoury! I did not mean to come across as a Karen. I shouldn't have said that. I have no right to assume anything about people that I know nothing about and from whom I have been far removed all my life. But just know that we are for you and we have your back. This is not just because of Amethyst. But from the get go, Mason struggled with his choice to let you into our lives and it was more as a result of that inner nudge why he met with you. It wasn't because of your business savvy. There are tons of people lining up to do business with us. Also, I believe that it is this deep connection that pulled Amethyst to you as well. It wasn't just his error in judgment."

Mason says, "So let's just put a pause on this for now. We can pick up when Mel is home safely."

Again, that sense of embarrassment. I completely forgot that, that poor girl was still out there somewhere. Maybe, even fighting for her life.

There is more awkward silence, thankfully, Mason gets a call and leaves the room for a bit while Val stares out the window.

After a few minutes, she says almost to herself, "He is so badly broken now, I don't know if anyone will be able to reach into his soul and pull him out."

I question, "Who is Val?"

She whispers, "Amethyst."

She proceeds to inform me of Amethyst's break from reality. Who can blame him? I wish I could take a break from reality. I feel great compassion for him and the Whiley family; my family.

"I cannot begin to explain how sorry I am. Val."

She waves me off and says, "What's done is done! Now we have to find a way to pick up all the many and various broken pieces and move on. My mum used to say, *there's no point crying over spilt applesauce.*" At the sudden memory of her mum, she weeps quietly with such poise and dignity. I am compelled to go to her and hold her! But I don't! I don't know why, when that is the most human and natural thing to do! Have I lost touch with humanity so much that I now resist human urges? Oh, good God, help me.

Chapter Twenty-Five
The Discovery

"One of the greatest discoveries a man makes, one of his great surprises, is to find he can do what he was afraid he couldn't do." – Henry Ford

Mason

The call was from detective Friar; apparently, he has made some new discoveries about the case and he wants to meet with me in his office. I am petrified to go, let alone by myself as I know from his tone that it won't be good news. I can feel it my bones. I want to bring Val, but is not fair to her, I could bring Amoury but he is no condition to travel. Despite our recent heated discussion, I know that he is almost as broken as Amethyst. All you have to do is look in his eyes and everything he is feeling and not expressing is written there in those Whiley green eyes.

With a sigh, I tell him I am on my way. I pop back in the room only to find Val in tears and Amoury looking more defeated than he has looked all day. I go to her and take her in my arms. I hate to leave but I must go; duty calls. This has always been my greatest fear as head of the Whiley clan that I would be called upon to take appropriate action in very unpleasant circumstances and really it doesn't get any more distressing than this. I tell them that I have to meet with the detective, I make a hasty retreat before I divest myself of my raw emotions.

I stop by the section of the hospital that Amethyst is in. By now they have him sedated. Who knew that when I was meeting with him this morning – as frustrating as it was – was the last time that I would see him lucid in a while. He seems this should read to be resting comfortably. I take his right hand in mine, hold it for a bit and then kiss his forehead. I feel such love and compassion for him that I have to fight the tears which have been threatening all day. I can't help but muse aloud, 'Why did you have to do this to yourself, little bro, when there was absolutely no need for any of this?' I would stay longer but duty is calling me. A duty that I would not wish upon my worst enemy.

I step outside the cold, unfriendly, hospital building leaving the strong smell of disinfectant and sickness behind. It is raining now; a slow and steady rain. I look up at the looming posture of the building and I am forced to make a quick escape. I know I am just fleeing one malevolent building to enter the next. When I woke up this morning, a police station is not where I thought that I would be spending my evening.

I walk into another yet another cold and menacing building, this one not as sanitised. There is a strong smell of sweat and dust. I introduce myself and very quickly, I am brought into the detective's office. A tiny cubicle with very outdated and uncomfortable furniture. It might be my mind, but I see the officers around me stealing looks at me. I steel myself for the onslaught. For the first time since we met, I guess with a view to distract myself, I take a good look at the detective. He is about forty-five but looks like he is sixty-five years old. He has a paunch resembling a kangaroo's pouch. He has deep-set light brown eyes and his complexion appears ashy. He has high-cheek bones, a tiny scar, just above his left eye. I assume that he collected that in the line of duty.

He clears his throat and we simultaneously sigh. He looks and me and looks away, as if to fortify himself. He begins,

"Thanks for coming, Mr Whiley…"

I interrupt, "Mr Whiley was my father, please call me Mason."

He smiles awkwardly, as if it is a new experience for him and continues.

"I am afraid that I have really bad news for you Mr… Mason. We have made some discoveries over the last few days, not what we were hoping for, but these things happen sometimes."

At this last comment, he pauses and looks out his tiny window. The rain is coming down heavier than before but not quite a torrential downpour. I see that it has gotten dark. I have so many memories of my sister. I remember when she was born, her first day of kindergarten, I was mad because I had to go with her. I remember her first day at high school, her first crush, her first heartbreak. I remember how the sun shone on her face when she told me about her first true love and her disappointment when she was commandeered not to marry him. I remember she brought her twins home from the hospital. I also fondly remember that when she just started to talk, at about two years ole, she used to call me *Mase* before she couldn't say my full name; even now she sometimes calls me that. This brings me back to the ugliness of the present situation at hand.

Detective Friar continues.

"It seems like Finley was mixed up in a whole lot of mess and somehow, his drug dealing associates followed him to your house that day and shot him."

"So, what does this have to do with my sister?"

"I'm getting to that. We found two phones on his body, a burner phone and another phone. We were not able to get anything from the burner, but on his regular phone we were able to access a series of text messages that he had been sending to his 'friends'. A few days before the incident, he had advised them that, 'Something big was going down at Emersyn. Soon. Just be patient, after that I will be able to pay you soon.' Those were his exact words. Do you care to elaborate on that, Mason?"

"I would but I have absolutely no clue what he could be talking about. I've never even met the man."

I need to know how much he knows before I proceed to say anything about Amethyst's and Amoury's involvement.

"Anyways, apparently whatever happened the day your sister disappeared they followed him to Emersyn, shot him there and abducted your sister."

"So where is she now? Did you find her?"

At this he sighs, looks weary and continues, looking like a beaten man, but quickly puts on his professional demeanour again.

"From his contacts, we were able to pull some names and in our pursuance of this lead, we *met* with a few of them. Some we know on a first name basis, if you know what I mean and others are new to the fray; in a manner of speaking. One, Jeffrey Lenstra, gave us a full confession. Like I said, he was new to the scene so he was quick to lawyer up and seek to make a deal. Through his lawyer, he told us that…"

"Detective, quit stalling! Please let me know what happened to my sister. I don't much care about anything or anyone else at this point in time. I just need to know if she's alive and when can I see her. Plus, I am a big boy, you don't need to sugar-coat things for me."

Friar sighs again.

"I'm getting to that, Mason, I just need to detail the facts in the case as we have them, just be patient."

"It seems like all I've been these days is patient. I need some answers and I NEED THEM RIGHT NOW!"

I really didn't mean to shout but I just need to no!

"Well then, Lenstra said that she died."

He pauses here and for the first time looks me dead in the eye.

"I am really sorry to tell you this! I wish it was otherwise."

"How?" I whisper this time.

"Well, it seems like they hit Finley over the head with a weapon of some kind and stuffed her in the trunk of a car…"

I am on autopilot now. I speak in a quiet monotone voice, a whisper.

"She's severely claustrophobic so she died in the trunk of the car."

"Yes, as far as we are able to ascertain. My men are right now out looking for the car."

"They discovered that she was dead and they just left her there."

"Yes, I'm afraid so. Apparently, they had intended to hold her hostage, seek a ransom and leave her at an obscure location with directions on how to find her. From the looks of things, they had no intentions of killing her as she meant more to them alive than dead."

"So that makes it better then… seeing that their intentions were honourable."

"No, Mr Whiley, I mean, Mason. That's not what I meant. Of course, they will be prosecuted to the fullest extent of the law. No two ways about that, sir. But I am just giving you the facts, as they appear in the case."

"I see!"

"You say, you have never meant the man; Finley. Yet, we are confused about how he came to be on your property, sir. Not just on the property, but in the mountain. Wouldn't he of necessity have to go through the front gate which is secure? I don't mean to be harsh, but somehow, Finley gained access to your property and his cronies were able to follow him there and that's exactly how they gained access to your sister."

"Detective, thanks for all you've done! I have to leave now. I need to inform my family of what has happened before they hear it from anyone else. I'll answer your questions at some other time. As soon as you have located her body, please let me know."

"Oh of course. We will need you to ID the body as well. And again, I am so sorry for how things have turned out. I truly wish that things were different; that I was giving you better news."

"I understand."

"Also, I know you have to go but the John Doe that was discovered in the mountain, it turns out that because of the cool temperatures in the mountain, the body was very well preserved. And based on the DNA we collected from you, it turns out that he is a close relative of yours. Also, he was wearing a jacket that does not seem to be his, it contains DNA that only partially matched his DNA. It could have belonged to a cousin or a half sibling."

I am not really paying attention but I think he believes one of our relatives was murdered by another relative. I almost laughed out loud. This day could not get anymore ludicrous; my sister died at the hands of her abductors and our relative died at the hands of another relative. I thanked him; although, I don't know why and left. He promised to call me as soon as he knows anything else.

By some means, maybe muscle memory, I make it home in the rain. I hate driving in the rain. Everyone is waiting there for me; even Amoury. Apparently, he was well enough to come home. Well everyone except Amethyst. I sigh and look at all their faces anticipating the worse but expecting the best. By now it is raining all kinds of wild animals outside. The rhythm of the rain used to be soothing for me but not tonight; tonight, nothing will comfort me, not even Mauve who is right next to me stroking my right arm. I have never; loved her more than I love her now, just the warmth of her presence is appreciated. I waste no time on preliminaries, I don't have the energy. In a quiet voice I tell them, "Mel is dead. Some guy confessed his involvement and they are out now looking for the car she was abducted in. Apparently, she suffocated in the trunk of a car. Also, the John Doe found in the mountain is one of our relatives who was apparently killed by another relative."

At the sound of these words, coming from my own voice, it is too much. The tears which have been threatening all day come gushing out of my face, much like the rain drumming on the roof. I am happy for the comfort of my wife's arms. She embraces me, like she does with our children when they have hurt themselves. I hear others crying around me, there is anger as well (as expected) but tonight, I am not going to attend to any of that. I am just going to mourn the loss of my sister, the loss of my mum and even our relative buried years earlier without a proper send off.

Tonight, I weep for the loss of these people who I hold dear. Tonight, I choose to forget everything else and focus on my loss. I believe that I owe it to myself to grieve properly, to sit in and with my pain, to let pain have her way with me; massaging my ego until it becomes pliable. It is only then that healing can begin once pain has done her job and left her mark.

****

Amoury

I hear what Mason is saying yet I don't want to hear it and I don't want to believe it. Once again, I feel like an intruder on their private pain. A pain that I have unwittingly contributed to. I wish I had stayed in the hospital tonight, just one more night to get my bearings back. But here I am, in the middle of the saddest scene that any human could be privy to. I see Val crying again, not with the quiet dignity of earlier but the piercing cry of a wounded animal. This time, I do go to her, hold her and she lets me. At least I am not uselessly standing around. At least I am helping. Mason has dissolved into a puddle of despair, a shell of himself. Nothing of his confidence visible; only raw emotions that seem contagious and is like an untamed virus that is spreading throughout the room and everywhere the virus touches is met with tears or anger.

I close my eyes as if to shut out the despair and prevent myself from being infected with the virus. However, I am a second too late because the tears come gushing down and I have lost control of myself of my will and my self-control.

Chapter Twenty-Six
The Obsequies

"A time to weep, and a time to laugh; a time to mourn, and a time to dance." –
Ecclesiastes 3:4 (KJV)

Val

This has been another trying and traumatic week. They finally found my sister's decomposing body. I have been crying all week. I don't even know how we're going to get through this funeral today. We are burying three of our relatives, Mum, Mel and apparently our great, great, great, Uncle Lawrence. At least they will be together and with the other family members buried in the family plot. Uncle Lawrence actually appeared to me a few nights ago. He said something really weird.

He said, "Check Amoury's blood."

I can't even begin to imagine what that means. I don't even have the strength. Maybe, I was just overthinking the fact that Detective Friar said that he was killed by a relative.

This has got to be the saddest day of my whole entire life. I don't even know how Mason is doing. He was the one who had to identify the body. Thankfully, he has Mauve. We still haven't told Amethyst. He is still in the hospital being treated. The doctors say he is responding well to treatment, a combination of meds and therapy. He is on meds so he is on the mend. Everyone is worried that this news about Mel will finish him. No one has the heart to be mad at him, we're not even angry at Amoury, they are being punished by their own conscience every day. Plus, Amoury has been so helpful, we cannot remember a time when he was not around. But we are working with a wonderful medical team so we're hoping that he will get through this. He keeps asking if we've heard anything about Mel; each time we go we have to lie to him and put on a brave face that all will be well. I have decided that I am never going back there, not when I have to lie to him. Every time we tell him not yet, he seems so hopeful. I can't bear to look him in the face. How did this happen to our family? When did we become so fractured?

It does help that Cora is back with the kids and she's being a dutiful wife, visiting him every day. I can't help but think, what might have happened if she had been here all along. Mason says, no point in hurting myself with the *what ifs* and Amoury agrees. In all honesty, this might not have happened if Amoury hadn't gotten involved in the first place; but on the other hand, I don't even know how I would have managed without him either. He's been a tower of strength and like I said, he is suffering in his own way. As it turns out, he is a man of great conscience. All we can do now is pray for the best outcome for all involved.

Cora is suffering as well. She carries a guilt that is always etched on her face. She has lost her best friend, her husband and the father of her children is so badly fractured that there is no telling whether he will ever be whole again.

She keeps asking everyone who will listen, "Is all this my fault? Could I possibly have prevented this disaster if I were present?"

The last time we spoke I had to ask, "Cora, why did you travel so much with the kids? Don't you think that in some way, this would have affected your marriage, affected your husband?"

She said with her eyes brimming with tears, "Amethyst never complained. So, I thought this was what he wanted. I thought us being away gave him an opportunity to work without being disturbed?"

I went on to ask her, "Wasn't being separated hard on you as well?"

She thought for a while and then answered quietly.

"My mum always said that marriage requires sacrifice and each situation is different. So, I honestly thought that this separation was the sacrifice that I was being called upon to make."

As Amethyst's only sister, I had to ask, "I'm sorry but I have to ask. But did you ever love my brother, I mean really love him?"

At this she stood up and anger flashed in her beautiful face but not for long as grief as rendered her emotionally exhausted.

She says with her bottom lip quivering,

Of course, I loved and still love your brother. I know you might think that my behaviour over the last little while has certainly not shown that but for sure without a doubt; I love him. He is the best thing that ever happened to me. Sure, sometimes he can be testy, but that's all part and parcel of his brilliance. I have always admired his work ethic and the way his brain works. So yes, I do love him, now more than ever. I intend to spend the rest of my life, taking care of him, loving him back to his former glory. Amethyst will rise again like a phoenix, advancing from the ashes of its ancestor. Amethyst will ascend from the ashes of this his old self and he will experience a rebirth like no other. He will be better than he has ever been. Plus, having the children near is good for him. I don't always take them, but the few times when I did, the doctors said, it made a world of difference. Amethyst will rise again! We will be fine!

The last sentence was said with so much conviction, it brought fresh tears to my eyes. I was reassured that all this comes from a place of love. Plus, Cora has always been so confident that I can't help but buy into her rose petal vision; her faith in Amethyst's recovery is certainly contagious, so much so that I will myself to completes the idea believe it. While her passion is commendable, I do have my doubts based on the body of evidence in front of me but I really hope that she is correct. It would be a double tragedy if we lost both him and Mel as well.

I guess time will tell.

****

Mason

This has been the week from hell. First, Mama dies while Mel is missing. Eventually, we discover that she had been abducted by some low-life based on a plan that Amethyst and Amoury had set in motion. Then finally last week Friday, Friar calls me to give me the low down on what has happened and told me more than likely Mel is dead. By Saturday afternoon, I was back at the station to identify my sister's body. That part I was not going to face alone so I brought the whole tribe, Amoury included because he's inextricably linked to us now, whether or not he was family. Of course, it helps that he is family; DNA evidence has confirmed this.

I have not said this to anyone in the family yet but I had to be clear in my own mind first that he is indeed a Whiley, it was the responsible and prudent thing to do. Plus, from that DNA sample we also discovered that Amoury is very closely linked to the person who might have killed Uncle Lawrence since their

DNA is a closer match than mine. This again, I have not told anyone. I figured that I would wait until after the service to tell Amoury, I might tell Val as well but most certainly no one else.

Sadly, Amethyst cannot be here with us. He is still badly broken. Despite the optimism of his doctors and Cora, based on how he is now, I cannot see him ever being the same again. Every time I think of my baby brother in the hospital, under restraints, sometimes depending on his mood, yelling at the world, I feel a pain running down my right arm. People say, after one goes through an ordeal, it is inevitable that he will never be the same but I sense that Amethyst is going to be so far removed from himself that he might be unrecognisable even to himself and that is what keeps me up at nights. It is not the change per se because I have accepted and embraced the fact that change is inevitable but it is the sheer magnitude of the change. I am just afraid that we will never be able to have access to his intellect ever again.

Ultimately, I had to give in and tell Friar about Amethyst and Amoury's intentions. I was grateful that he said that based on how everything had unfolded and the death of Finley then they couldn't be charged with anything based on the chain of evidence that unfolded. Their plan was not actually executed and they couldn't be held accountable for Finley's dealings; most importantly, they had no knowledge of Finley's business dealings.

Friar said, "Sadly, is just a series of unfortunate events, that Ms Whiley inadvertently became entangled with."

That doesn't make it hurt any less but I guess it is some comfort to know that my cousin and brother will not be liable for my sister's death.

We went in to identify her body and I have been struggling against the unfairness of it all – seeing her like that, ashen pale and stiff. I cannot get it out of my head, the thought of how horrified, how deeply petrified she must have been. It hurt more to see that her legs were so badly bruised and all her beautiful nails broke; as a result of her attempt to escape the confines of the trunk of a car. I shudder every time I think that if Amoury had not found Finley's corpse that car might have been her coffin in a watery grave. My sister should have been here today to mourn and celebrate Mama's life. We should not be called upon to bury her with mum and Uncle Lawrence.

It is a bright sunny day, the day of our triple funeral service. The day does not belie any of the sadness of today. The birds are chirping, performing their glide show across the sky, the flowers are bobbing their heads to the wind band.

It is just an all-round beautiful day, one that Mel would have enjoyed to the fullest. The sadness is palpable. By the time we gather in the private section of our local church, there isn't a dry eye in the room. The floral arrangement is spectacular but still does nothing to mute the pain of sad farewell.

We sing all of Mama's favourite hymns, *When the Role is Called up Yonder, The Comforter Has Come*; normally, I find the hymns, any hymn, quite comforting but not today. And from the look reflected on all the faces, no one else is comforted either. My oldest son and Amethyst's oldest son read the lessons although I couldn't focus on anything they had to say.

Just before the ceremony, I am called to eulogise my mum, Val eulogises Uncle Lawrence (from notes found in the archives) and Emery eulogises Mel. I start with a quote by Thomas Campbell, *to live in hearts we leave behind is not to die*. This is true. Our relatives will always live on in our heart; however, it is still a woefully melancholy affair that no one wanted to partake in but here we are. Although my role was to celebrate Mum, I couldn't help talking about my sister. Sure, I miss Mum immensely but Mum had lived a long and wonderful life, Uncle Lawrence had been long dead but my sister was, oh so young; she had so much of life yet to live. She had so much to give, so much to contribute, so much to live for – her life never should have ended this way. Just thinking about that I couldn't stop the tears from gushing out of my eyes like water gushing over a precipice. As the head of the family, I know I should be comforting everyone but not today. I guess a huge part of my sadness is because with all the money and resources at my disposal, I couldn't save her, I couldn't give her life back.

I thought the service was misery personified but the graveside was unbearable. Everyone lost it; even Gabe. It was too much, too finally. The pastor had to dig deep into his bag of tricks to console us. I missed most if not all that he said at the service but at the graveside he said something that later I called back to memory to comfort myself. He said,

Mourn if you must but not for too long.
Weep if you will but not for too long.
For the dead needs time themselves to mourn their loss, loss of a life, a dream, a goal.
Should you choose to be too long in your mourning, they continue to weep and mourn with you. So, you keep them back from moving on to the next season

179

in their life by holding them hostage with your tears because tears are a language that is tangible for both the quick and the dead.

I don't know if this is true but I feel that deep in my soul I must temper my mourning to let my loved ones go. How horrible it would be to be kept in a state of perpetual sadness by the people who love you the most, intentions though favourable, plant you firmly, fetter you to Earth's realm when heaven should be your new domain. Then, I think about Uncle Lawrence who must have been fettered to his shallow grave for years because his siblings must have mourned him both night and day.

It is so calamitous that one tragedy opens the door to the next and then the next and pretty soon, one is left with a fleet of traumatic events. The other piece to this never-ending tragedy is Timothy Sanderson. We endeavoured to keep the ceremony private just among us. But somehow Timothy Sanderson discovered that Mel had died and he was inconsolable. No one had the heart to turn him away because his sorrow was just as real as ours; even made more palpable because of all those missing years. He walked in during Emery's eulogy and wept for the whole service. It is amazing how much the twins have grown to look like him.

Apparently, he had been keeping tabs on her all these years. He never stopped loving her, never gave up on her, on us. It is only a pity he was not around when she was being abducted. Anyways, it's for the best, because then, the twins would have lost both parents in one terrible ordeal. It was heart-breaking to see his raw emotions on display. He too must be weeping for the life that might have been. I can't help but wonder what might have happened if their romance was allowed to bloom. Would we be burying her today? Would she have been so attached to Amethyst that she would do anything for him or would she have been committed to her own husband?

That and so many other things we will never know.

Chapter Twenty-Seven
The Coalesce

Seven Months Later

"You don't choose your family. They are God's gift to you." – Desmond Tutu

Amoury

After the storm, there is a calm. After those particular weeks from hell, I can finally breathe again. My focus is different now because I now have so much more to live for and process. I saw this quote on an Instagram post and it speaks volumes to me, *I went looking for revenge but I found peace.* Also, not only did I find peace, I found a new family that loved and accepted me unconditionally; more than anyone else ever did, not even my family that I grew up with. They have forgiven me so much, accepted me fully and even seem to understand my idiosyncrasies that have marked me as weird all my life. Val has become a true tower of strength over the last little while. I don't even remember what my life used to be like before her.

I keep thinking that, if they wanted to be vindictive, the Whileys could have spun a tale that would have sent me to prison for life. They certainly have the evidence and the motive. Yet they didn't. Mason sought to protect me as much as he protected Amethyst. I am eternally grateful. When I asked him about this when we last spoke, he said, "Amoury, as a family, we have suffered enough losses. We have lost too many of our most valued resources so let's just not look back at what happened. Let's look ahead and see what happened for what it really is; a lesson in being prudent. Let's look to the future and not the past. The future holds so much bright hope for tomorrow but the past embodies so much sadness and loss. I just want to forget it and do everything in my power to correct whatever I can of the past."

That Mason is certainly very wise and poetic; no wonder he is in charge of the Whiley fortune. It is definitely in very capable hands.

In addition, Mason told me that he secretly had my DNA tested. I couldn't even be mad at him because it was the sensible thing to do – as he would say, 'the most prudent thing to do'. If I were in his place, I most certainly would have done that. Turns out, that the DNA found on Uncle Lawrence's jacket might have belonged to Laika and quite possibly Laika might have been responsible for his death. The coroner ruled the cause of death as an affixation. I am almost a hundred percent certain that Laika must have done it; especially, because Uncle had told Val to 'check my blood'. Why else would Uncle be wearing Laika's jacket? Based on how society was stratified, I don't think that they were that close. Plus, based on the things recorded in the Whiley archives, Laika was by no means a saint. But one thing is for sure; he might have been only half but, he through his actions has demonstrated that, he was most definitely a Whiley. This leads me to wonder though, *Could Laika have been a serial killer? Could it be possible that he had become so hopeless, so desperate that he had resorted to murder?*

The plain truth is; I can't even judge him. Look at all I had done in the name of a righteous cause. Moreover, like Val said, he must have had his reasons. Now whether or not they were justified, he must have felt that that was his only option.

This weekend Mason has invited me, my siblings and cousins to a family gathering. This is way too cool. I've not had an opportunity to communicate with Mason a lot over the last little while (he is always too busy) but when we do speak, it is meaningful. On the other hand, I have kept in close contact with Val. Just thinking about her makes me smile and I feel like I would climb Mount Diablo for her; barefoot. Everyone seems to be healing. It will take a while but at least they have a whole house full of family members to lean on. Plus, us their new cousins. Hopefully, Mel's senseless death will not be in vain. Hopefully, it will facilitate whatever change is necessary and appropriate. I really feel like all of us should grow from this.

The other exciting thing to come out of this is that, I have made arrangements to meet with my other mixed cousins here in Shrove. Apparently, many of them still live in Shrove. Most of them are doing really well for themselves. Prior to meeting me, Mason and his siblings never mixed with them as they moved in different spheres. But while it wouldn't be prudent to just randomly accept all of them; at least, little by little a bond is being created between the white side and the black side of my family. This is indeed huge, when I had initiated my plans,

I never imagined that anything like this could have happened but I am grateful that it has.

One thing I have learned about people is that, we all want to be included, we all want to be a part of something that is indeed bigger than ourselves and sometimes just the mere fact that we are considered a part of a whole is enough. Over the centuries wars have been fought and lost because people felt like they had been excluded; whether they were right or being legal in their claims fundamentally that was their main conclusion.

****

Val

All the unpleasantries of the last few months have certainly weighed heavily on me and tested my emotional strength. I am still drained; however, while Mel has not made an appearance – I have been hoping she would – I take comfort from a recurring dream I have been having. In my dream, it is like when we were kids and we used to play near or under the watchful eyes of Buddy, her favourite game was hide and seek. She is dressed in her a light pink summer dress, with tiny green petals on in, with her hair pulled back in a ponytail. Rays of sunshine are wafting in behind her, she looks like she is one with the light. She is hiding among the branches and when I get a glimpse of her, she mostly has a huge smile on her face. She looks angelic. At some points in the dream, I hear her beautiful laughter, it is like the proverbial music to my ears but at those times, I don't see her. However, I hear her beautiful, raspy voice mixed in with the wind.

I take this as a sign that she is at peace, that she has finally found contentment – that she is finally at peace to make her own choices and follow her own path. Because, we all knew that over the last little while, Mel has been extremely unhappy. She barely used to smile at anyone so I find this dream extremely comforting. Maybe, just maybe this is her way of assuring us that she has transitioned well and we shouldn't worry about her so much. I have even shared this dream with Amoury and he agrees that it is a good sign that she is finally content. I'm so grateful to Amoury, he's been such a tower of strength.

We talk every single day and the more I talk with him is the more I love him. We've only shared our relationship status with Mason. At first, I was severely stressed because we are cousins which might be problematic. However, Mason argued that while we are cousins, we are so far removed that even Amoury's

DNA is slightly different – he eventually, shared with me that he got Amoury's DNA tested to see if we are really cousins. We've been talking about getting married but we are in no rush. I know for sure that Amoury is the one my soul loves so even if we wait for another ten years, it is always going to be him.

****

Amethyst

"I have tried prudent planning long enough. From now on I'll be mad." – *Rumi*

Things haven't been the same since my Mel went away.

How could this have happened? One day she's here, we go in search of Chloe in the mountains and then she goes missing! God damn Chloe!

I have imagined how she must have felt all the time, at the end, when she knew that death was near. I am pretty sure she knew her death was near and she knew I was the cause; oh she must have cursed me with her dying breath.

I wake up every day expecting to see her. I wake up every day hoping that this is will be the day I will awaken from this hellish nightmare. But that never happens. I wake up to this confined space every day; the same four bland walls. These dreary walls with the smell of antiseptic burning my nostril.

I do see Cora though all the time and my kids occasionally. Sometimes I wonder if she is really here or her presence is a part of the illusion; while at other times, she is so far away, I can't touch her; I can't hold her hands like before. At those times, I try touching her with my mind but even that doesn't work; too disconnected over the years. On days when she brings the kids, it is both refreshing and disturbing – two conflicting emotions fighting for supremacy. I really don't want them to see me like this because I have unintentionally surrendered my Armani suits for hospital garb; certainly not the most flattering wear.

I don't think I have seen them (my kids I mean not my suits) in a long time but then again maybe I have; who knows. I can never be certain of anything these days. To think that all these years, this is exactly what I have wanted, no needed, my wife and kids near yet I kept driving her away saying *I am way too busy*. It must have made her feel like a visitor in my life occupying a space where my wife should be. Turns out that I am not that busy anymore. Look at that! And the

184

world keeps spinning on its axis, the sun still shines, the stars still come out in their time and the seasons will go on as before without me; without any input from me. We must always endeavour to hold our loved ones in close proximity to our heart.

All I do these days is just lie around, feeling either dazed or confused, my thoughts muddled or empty, numb, just dead inside. Sometimes a nurse, or Cora or Val or Mason pushes me in a wheelchair to the hospital garden. They talk about the tranquillity of the grounds, the flowers and their smell, the birds but all I see is either oblivion, true nothingness, a void never to be filled or blood and broken bones as I stare straight ahead.

I am constantly weak and groggy from the meds. Meds that I will probably need for the rest of my life. The irony is, as far as I can remember, I have never been ill a day in my life. I have been told that it's been seven long months since Mel left us. Most of the events after she went missing have been a blur. I have been medicated to infinity and the shock of everything keeps me off kilter. However, I do remember that it was through my poor planning that my sister, my twin died. As much as Mason tries to convince me that I could not have foreseen the events that transpired but I did set them into motion, didn't I? So, doesn't that make me even two thirds responsible? Really, I am her brother, bound by love and duty to keep her safe, a sacred responsibility which is not given to many and should; therefore, be held in the highest esteem.

All my siblings have come by to visit my pale, overly sanitised, sparse room even Gabe. I have grown to abhor their visits. I am upset before and after each visit. Dr Levi (my doctor now) says it's because their presence reminds me of what I have loved and lost. Personally, I think it's their abject pity. The only person who seems to be unchanged is Gabe whose habitual apathy is both heart-warming and appealing. Naturally, they blame me and why wouldn't they? I blame me. If I hadn't been so covetous none of this would have happened. Doesn't the Bible warn against the sin of covetousness? I'm sure it does. I'll have to ask Val the next time she visits; if I remember. I am pretty sure she will know.

I don't know why I ever had any dealings with Finley, that felon. Mason says that the people responsible for Mel's demise – that's what he calls it, demise – will be punished to the fullest extent of the law and he is going to do everything in his power to keep my name out of their mouths. Good old, sturdy, prudent Mason always so reliable. It doesn't matter much to me, none of that will bring my sister back. In fact, nothing matters anymore. In my coherent moments, my

185

heart hurts so much that I think I will die a slow and painful death. I keep telling them that it hurts but of the various meds and techniques available to them in this wretched place, none of them can help me.

There is no medication to heal a broken heart.

****

Mason

My whole heart is still broken knowing that my sister died senselessly. At the funeral service, I encouraged everyone to live their lives intentionally to honour her memory. I am hoping that much good will come of her untimely passing. So far, we've set up the Melisandre Whiley Foundation for young women who have been the victim of a crime perpetuated by someone under the influence of any type of narcotics. Also, through Whiley Inc. we have donated money to the Special Victims Unit at the local precinct.

Most importantly, Amethyst is healing slowly but surely. I finally told him about Mel a month after and he had to be sedated for a week. We didn't think he was going to make it. He was beside himself with guilt and grief. When he was finally lucid, both him and Amoury had a long talk and that seemed to help a great deal. I guess they will both carry this grief and guilt with them forever. Amoury is such a huge asset to this family. Everyone is happy that he came *home* but no one is happier than Val. My little sister is finally in love. They do make a beautiful couple after all.

While I am sad that I have lost both of my parents, an advantage of that is the fact that the old folks with their very archaic ideas are not around to ruin this for them with their antediluvian ideology and expectations. Fundamentally, it is these expectations which have caused hardships over the years. Mum would have had a coronary if she were still here and saw Val and Amoury embracing each other. That would have ignited too much guilt in their relationship so like Val usually says, '*All things work together for good.*' It doesn't matter how bad it seems, how negative, if you look closely enough, there is some good in it. Sometimes you have to be patient as well to see the good emerge.

Speaking about couples, Cora and Amethyst are doing well. Amelia and Emery have made amends and are actively engaging in counselling; while, Everest and Andira are expecting and I've never seen them being so cordial to each other. Gabe is still being Gabe but in fairness, he is a lot more social. Chloe is still Chloe but she grew a bit. Mauve and I have never been closer and our sex life has never been better. We all learned first-hand that life can be unpredictable; in that, one day you're here and the next day you're not.

Moreover, I decided that it was time for Timothy to know that he is the father of the twins. He wept uncontrollably but I surmised that those were tears of joy. He said he always felt a deep connection to them. I guess just like mine and Val's reaction to Amoury blood ties don't lie. Deep calls unto deep. I have to admit though, that over the last little while, I have had some really difficult conversations but the one I had with Timothy was the most heart rending.

He kept asking me, "Why did it have to come to this, Amoury? Why did it take her leaving? I am absolutely useless without her! My life is forever changed."

I told him that I know and he rightfully said, "You don't know. How could you know?"

He is right; though, how could I know?

Everyone agreed that it was the right thing to do. He lives here now, because after all, the twins are Whileys, we can't just allow them to leave. It took a while to convince him that if he wanted to be a father to them, he had to move into Emersyn. I think it's bittersweet him being here and Mel being absent but even in her absence her presence is still felt. It is first seen in the kids, in us, her brothers and sister and in Timothy's devotion to her memory. Gabe recently asked what will happen should Timothy decide to get married, would his wife be welcomed here? To be honest, I don't have an answer to that. We will cross that bridge when we get there. In the meantime, the twins are happy to at least have one parent left and for now that's more than enough.

Indeed, Amoury has brought the wind of change to Emersyn. It happened at the right time with the right players. I have a lot of regret about how it happened but I am finally grateful that it happened on my watch. This is a huge part of our history and I was here to play assist. But one thing I know for sure, us Whiley's are made of sterner stuff, so we are all going to be fine; as long as we just continue being prudent.

Amoury and I had a talk about *white privilege*, which he had hinted at while he was in the hospital when Val had brought up slavery in Africa. This is not a term that I am familiar with but he broke it down for me. He said, imagine that your father built a bridge connecting Emersyn to the rest of the town. Over the years the town grew, your father eventually dies, as all who lives must die. After his death, the people in the town ask that you move the bridge to a little bit over to the right which would give everyone equal access to the bridge so that everyone will have equal opportunities to use the bridge and carry on with their daily life. This would improve everyone's life in equal part. However, I decide not to, to honour my father's wishes, to keep everything just so. So, in effect, I have denied other people who are not Whileys, the right to improve themselves, just to honour an outdated way of thinking. Amoury says, in a nutshell, that's white privilege. The bridge is a metaphor for the systems that have been left in place by our forefathers, that keep other people out and us in the lead because we want to maintain our position in the world.

Talk about an eye opening experience! I get it now! I, in my position as head of the Whileys will endeavour to help all my half cousins. I've decided that while I cannot help everyone, I will start with them and see where that leads. Obviously, over the years they have been mistreated and denied equal opportunities as result of their skin colour; which they have nothing to do with, they have no control over that. I feel like and injustice has been committed and it is my destiny to make amends as much as it lies in my power. Some of them still live in squalor while we live in luxury. At some point, we have to accept our place in the world and the reality of our responsibility.

We all learned some very harsh lessons in being prudent over the last little while. Lessons that we will not soon forget, that in and of itself is a blessing.

****

AVAILABLE NOW
ZIMERA
TURN THE PAGE NOW FOR AN EXCERPT

ZIMERA

a novel by

Kareen Samuels

Chapter Twenty-Eight
Cyril's Nightmare

It always starts this way, a dream about shadows – being lost in the shadows. In the tradition of dreams it quickly escalates into utter darkness. Darkness that's so thick that you can almost touch it. As a matter of fact, that's the natural inclination to reach out and touch it; to hold it up to your face. Eventually, you do get used to the darkness especially after having this dream a few times. Ultimately, the free fall is frightening and you scream as loudly as you can but then you realise that you are all alone and just like in waking moments, no one, absolutely no one is coming to help, no one is coming to your rescue. That's singularly one of the most petrifying thoughts that can afflict a human being, the deep sense of isolation which leads to alienation.

At first, I just let it happen – the free fall I mean – which is both exhilarating and terrifying at the same time. Then, as falling becomes more familiar, I learn to play with the shadows, imagine faces and indiscreet objects as they pass me by.

On this particular night – that too – it is always at night. Why is it always at night? The free fall intensifies and for some other worldly reason, I can somehow sense that the ultimate purpose will be different tonight. A sense of deeper darkness and a falling away of everything I know to be true; to be real, to be true. Naturally, I fight as at other times, to rouse myself and put a halt to the free fall. Soon, it becomes obvious that all my old tricks are outdated, I am unable to sway my course and resistance is futile.

After struggling for a while, against everything that is rational and wholesome, I decide to go with it to see what happens. Again, I rely on the ordinary, to wake up before I hit rock bottom. Fortunately, this does not happen as I have an appointment with destiny, against my best judgment and natural proclivities. I brace myself for the inevitable splatter of my innards. Luckily, this doesn't happen either but the shadows and strange sounds loom in the distance, becoming bigger and louder. I attempt to cover my eyes and ears but there is just no escaping the onslaught; as that is both useless and difficult to accomplish in flight.

That's when I hear the word – mind you, in all my midnight rendezvous – there has always been words – from which I could discern implicit meanings, even when spoken in a foreign language. The resounding word of the night is ZIMERA. The peculiarity of the word is not in the word itself but how it is expressed – almost like an incantation – an omen. After this pronouncement, I am unable to process what I've heard, because the shadows materialise into unexpected images.

Previously, I just imagined their existence but it seems like all my dark imaginings have called them into sharp focus. Strange being a relative concept in my current situation, I mean images that I have seen before or in some way know of their existence, but chose to forget, appear with an added dimension of gruesomeness. For instance, there is that bat with red, translucent wings and talons, it turns into a cobra that wraps itself around me, an eagle suddenly makes an appearance, quickly swallowing the snake and they both disappear. A dead boy wrapped in yellow florescent light with wine, red blood dripping from a huge gash in his abdomen. I quickly turn away because I do not want to witness his organs spilling or capture his face. Most images are easily forgotten but for me, not faces.

Over the din of the moment, I hear a guttural sound and I wonder where it comes from. Soon, I discover the source of the disruption – it is me – I am the guttural sound. Based on the dryness and soreness of my throat I realise that I am making the sound. Suddenly, I feel myself being shaken unceremoniously and I check to see if it is the boy; thankfully, it isn't because I am awake. I am awake! Joyfully and jubilantly awake in my own bed, in my own room, in my own house not in some dungeon; soaking in perspiration, being embraced by my lifelong friend.

"Cyril, Cyril, Cyril! Wake up!"

"Are you OK?"

"Speak to me, man!"

My friend, Austin, came to dinner earlier and decided to sleep over! I forgot that I wasn't alone – not tonight. Usually, I am alone but Austin decided to sleep over. It was just like old times when we were growing up.

"I'm good, I'm good!"

I manage to stutter, tasting the rawness of my throat, fighting back bile and feeling the start of a migraine. He simultaneously strokes and hugs me as if I'm his child; despite my three years' difference in age.

I catch my breath and recover my voice.

"Can you please get me some water?"

Almost immediately, I hear the tap in the bathroom running and Austin is by my side again.

"What was that screaming about, man? It sounded like... like screams from hell."

Austin's turn to stutter.

I'm about to confide in him but suddenly I'm scared. *What if he thinks I'm going insane?*

"Ah it's nothing!" I say in my most convincing voice.

However, a slight quiver is not missed by my forever friend. I see him tense instinctively and move closer to place a protective arm on my shoulder. Never mind that this is the fifth week in a row that I've had at least a version of this dream once per week.

This dream has somehow deviated since the first occurrence. But I'm unable to process how because Austin is speaking to me again.

"That didn't sound or look like nothing! Your face was contorting as if mirroring the images! Signalling a fear that I've never seen before!"

I vehemently insist that I'm good. He looks at me accusingly but says nothing. I chime in quickly before he is able to challenge my words.

"I am just really tired so that's why I was dreaming in colour!"

I laugh loudly at my own sad joke which is my default reaction to any form of discomfort – laughter. Austin shakes his head as if to clear the images but seems genuinely relieved; although, he doesn't laugh along with me, not this time, which conveys to me his genuine concern and fear.

He says, "Are you sure you're going to be OK?"

More to appease him than anything else I suggest,

"You are welcome to sleep here, in my bed, if that makes you happy!"

He is caught off guard by this unusual request but quickly recovers. He states,

"OK, but if you as much as breathe on me too hard, I'll skin you alive!"

We both laugh out loud this time and pretend that we're having a typical evening. I tell him to leave the light on for good measure.

A grown man sleeping with the lights on. When did my life become so pathetic?

CPSIA information can be obtained
at www.ICGtesting.com
Printed in the USA
BVHW052115230623
666316BV00004B/130

9 781398 441651